London After Midnight

London After Midnight

An English Translation of the 1929 French Novelization of the Lost Lon Chaney Film

Edited, with a Preface and Afterword
by Thomas Mann

Translation of Lucien Boisyvon's
Londres Après Minuit
by Kieran O'Driscoll

BearManor Media
2018

Table of Contents

Preface

THE DISCOVERY OF THE NOVEL *Londres Après Minuit*, written by Lucien Boisyvon and published in France in 1929, gives fans of Lon Chaney yet another take on the most eagerly-sought of all lost films; it is another major source in addition to the many discussed in my previous book *London After Midnight: A New Reconstruction Based on Contemporary Sources* (BearManor Media, 2016). Boisyvon (1886-1967), who as author used only his last name as a kind of brand, was a prolific writer and newspaper critic, described in French biographical sources as "Auteur dramatique, publiciste, romancier," and "cinéphile." His novelization *Londres Après Minuit* is one of the Ciné-Volume series published by J. Ferenczi et Fils in Paris in the 1920s and '30s; the latter consisted of dozens of novelized version of contemporary films written by multiple authors. Boisyvon himself wrote at least nineteen film novelizations including those in other series such as *Les Grands Romans Films* and *Cinéma-Bibliothèque*. The catalog of the Bibliothèque Nationale, the national library of France, lists more than thirty books to his credit.

The last known copy of the 1927 *London After Midnight* film that he novelized in 1929 was destroyed in an MGM vault fire on May 13th, 1967; but a wide range of surviving sources tells us much about what was in it. This material includes a published shooting script and a full-length photoplay-edition novel based on it; a pressbook including a plot summary of the story; dozens of still photographs; numerous contemporary reviews; copyright registrations; the film editor's typed cutting continuity (a skeletal listing of every scene in the final film with all intertitles); music cue sheets to accompany the film; and an 11,000 word fictionized version of the film published in the British periodical *Boy's Cinema* at the time of the film's London release in 1928.

Two recent attempts to reconstruct the film must be added to the mix. The first is a book-format reconstruction by Philip J. Riley, *London After Midnight: A Reconstruction* (Cornwall Books, 1985; revised 2ⁿᵈ edition: BearManor Media, 2011). Film historian Riley used almost all of the surviving still photos from the film and arranged them in the order provided by the cutting continuity, including the original intertitles written by Joe Farnham. The second is a 2003 DVD version created by Rick Schmidlin and published by TCM Archives (Turner Classic Movies); its visual emphasis uses essentially the same still photos and intertitles, again arranged according to the plot sequence given by the cutting continuity but given "motion" by camera panning and zooming. An original musical score was created for this project. (The film's original music cue sheets were discovered only subsequently.)

The problems with these two reconstructions are that, first, there aren't enough surviving still photos to illustrate all of the scenes known (from the cutting continuity) to have been in the actual film; and this has required frequent re-use of many of the same shots, simply cropped or enlarged differently, at different places in the sequence. Second, the use of the cutting continuity – although it is indeed our best record of what was in the actual film – is problematic in itself because the plot of the story, as given therein, is simply incoherent. (This fact was noted by several contemporary reviews of the film.) In using that skeletal outline of the story's content, then, in conjunction with an inadequate pool of surviving still photos, both reconstructions were required to add additional explanatory intertitles of their own; and these, in both cases, have further exacerbated the original plot's existing problems.

Another way to imaginatively "reconstruct" the film, however, is through literary sources: fictionized versions of the film published with selected photos from it, sufficient to give readers a visual sense both of the characters' appearances and of the settings in which they move. Such literary stories can fill in much more of what is going on in a story than can be conveyed visually by the still photos and intertitles alone.

Up to now only two major literary versions of *London After Midnight* contemporary with the film have been known. The first is the afore-mentioned photoplay edition by Marie Coolidge-Rask (New York: Grosset & Dunlap, 1928; London: The Readers Library Publishing Company, 1928). This version of the story was based on an advance copy of the film's shooting script (published in the Riley volumes cited above), and completed before the film was released, in order to be marketed at the same time that the film appeared in theaters. (The February 15, 1928, copyright date of the American edition of the novel represents it registry in the U.S. Copyright Office; the book itself was available earlier to readers, at the time of the film's release on December 3, 1927.)

The main problem with the Coolidge-Rask fictionization is that the advance copy of the script that it is based on does not represent any of the subsequent and extensive editing that took place to produce the released version of the film; it is the latter version that is represented in the cutting continuity. The plot of the story, in going from the one version to the other, underwent major changes: the script has two murders, the continuity has one. The script has the Chaney character, Detective Burke, masquerade not only as the vampiric Man in the Beaver Hat but also as a "Colonel Yates" character – who is entirely deleted in the continuity, although Chaney's "Yates" make-up remains in the film as a different 'persona' of Detective Burke. This change in his physical appearance in the middle of the film makes the Burke character appear radically different from how he looks at the beginning and end – a striking alteration that is not well-explained in the continuity. Indeed, there are *many* other important discrepancies between the script and the continuity; these are discussed at length in my previous book, and need not be rehearsed in detail here.

The second surviving contemporary literary version of the story is an 11,000-word fictionization of the film published in the British magazine *Boy's Cinema* in December of 1928, the month of the film's release in London. The anonymous author of this photo-illustrated story very definitely follows the plot as given in the film's cutting continuity – unlike the Coolidge-Rask fictionization that follows the prior script. There is every indication that this author actually saw the film. (This story is reprinted in full in my previous book.)

Londres Après Minuit can now be added to the mix as the third contemporary literary fictionization of the story. This newly-discovered 32,500-word novelization of the film written in French in 1929 has now been ably translated into English by Kieran O'Driscoll of Ireland, whose talents have been previously used in BearManor Media's Palik Series of Jules Verne translations. This, too, is a contemporary "photoplay edition".

The most important introductory observation I can make about this version of the story is that it, too, follows the basic plot given in the cutting continuity – i.e., one murder rather than two; no "Col. Yates" character, etc. – and so its author must have seen the actual film. Unlike the *Boy's Cinema* writer, however, the French author evidently did not have access to any of the array of English language supplemental materials, i.e., the shooting script, the Coolidge-Rask novelization, the pressbook – or the *Boy's Cinema* version – with which to "fill in the holes" in the plot as given onscreen.

What this means is that he had only one source – his viewing of the film itself – to provide the basic plot to which he adheres. Given the incoherence of that plot, Mr. Boisyvon (like his *Boy's Cinema* counterpart) quite evidently recognized its problems. He then set about filling in the gaps, anomalies, and inconsistencies he was confronted with by making up his own "filler" material. The result is a story that adheres to the basic plot of the cutting continuity – and therefore to the plot of the now-missing film – but which is nonetheless very different from both of the previous literary fictionizations.

I don't want to provide spoilers here about the directions taken by this version of the story; I will discuss these in relation to the cutting continuity in the Afterword.

The only other known copy of *Londres Après Minuit*, apart from the one now in my possession, resides in the Bibliothèque Nationale de France. It is no wonder that this source has been overlooked by previous scholars (myself included): much like the *Boy's Cinema* version, it has been just as much "lost" as the actual film until its very recent rediscovery. A full presentation of it, for the first time in English, follows.

BOISYVON

London After Midnight

A Novel

Following the film as interpreted
by LON CHANEY
(*Metro-Goldwyn-Mayer*)

LONDON AFTER MIDNIGHT

Starring

LON CHANEY ....*Detective Burke.*

MARCELINE DAY.......................................*Lucile.*

AND

CONRAD NAGEL ....*Arthur Hibbs.*

Part One

A Man Is Killed

THE HONOURABLE Edward C. Burke was beginning the summing up of his investigation.

"I think," he said, "that there can be no possible room for doubt. Sir Roger Bradford was killed by a shot from a firearm. I am also sure it was a bullet fired from a *revolver* that caused his death. In a nutshell, all of that is perfectly clear: there was a gunshot; a man, lying dead on the ground, was discovered. There is nothing that can be done by us to alter those facts."

The sound of a sigh broke the heavy silence.

The sigh had emanated from the butler who was standing somewhat apart from the others, in a corner, modestly distancing himself from all of the other persons present at the detective's summing up of his investigation, and all of whom were members of the dead man's family.

Burke turned towards him and said to him, in an almost cheery tone of voice: "Rotten weather, isn't it, Williams?"

"Yes, Detective," came Williams' short, simple reply.

Williams always politely agreed with everyone, just as his professional duty required of him, but, in actual fact, and under the present circumstances, the detective's assertion couldn't be argued with.

Detective Burke smiled affably at Williams. The turbulence of the elements were actually of little concern to Burke, for he wasn't blessed with a romantic spirit.

"Yes indeed, my good friend, it's wretched weather we're having at the moment, but on the other hand, it isn't the weather I've come here to talk to you about."

Williams politely bowed his head, saying: "Yes, Detective."

He was prepared to make all possible concessions to decorum and politeness.

"Well," continued Burke, "since we need to talk a little bit about things that are of more direct, pressing concern to us, and so that we can get ourselves out of this blind alley in which we presently find ourselves, let me ask you, Williams: how long have you been a butler in the service of Sir Roger Bradford?"

Williams' reply was clear: "For twenty years, Sir."

"And tell me, Williams: you claim you didn't at all hear the gunshot that most probably caused the death of your master?"

"No, Sir, I heard nothing."

Burke frowned. "So why, then, did you come downstairs to this room immediately after the death occurred?"

Williams appeared a little ill at ease at this question. One might almost have thought that he was experiencing some difficulty in giving clear expression to this thoughts. He blinked, opened his mouth and closed it several times, before finally resolving to reply:

"Sir, I don't know what came over me. I had some sort of vague feeling, some sixth sense that something had happened to my master. It was as if some strange, supernatural force drove me to make my way down here, and I couldn't resist its power. It was I who discovered the body, in the very position that it currently occupies. I hope that there's nothing wrong with that, surely, Sir?"

Burke carefully, keenly looked the butler in the eye for a good thirty seconds, then said, in a gruff though not unkindly manner: "Hum! No, there's nothing wrong with any of that, but permit me to point out that it really *was* a strange presaging of disaster on your part – you don't happen to possess the gift of second sight, do you, Williams?"

The butler shook his head. "Nobody has ever told me any such thing, Sir! I'm an ordinary, respectable individual."

Burke gave the merest hint of a smile. "Sir James," he said, now bluntly addressing that gentleman, "you claim to have bid your cousin goodnight and to have left him alone here at eleven o'clock. Did you run into anybody after leaving him?"

Sir James thought about this question for a moment, searching his recollections, then shook his head. "No, I didn't see anyone; or at least I saw nobody unfamiliar to me; the only person I caught a glimpse of after having left Sir Roger, still alive at that point, was my nephew Arthur

Hibbs. He was reading in his bedroom, at my house, and I remained for a few moments in his company to ask him to lend me a certain work of philosophy that I was interested in consulting."

Burke frowned. "Ah!" said he, "so you saw your nephew?"

"I certainly did," replied Sir James, a little taken aback.

"He was reading, you say?"

"Yes!"

"And nothing about his manner or appearance seemed unusual?"

Sir James, wide-eyed, made no attempt to conceal the surprise he was feeling. Nonetheless, this question caused him some nameless anxiety and he couldn't help asking, in a stuttering voice: "Surely you don't suspect my nephew, Mr Burke?"

To which the detective sharply and drily retorted: "It's my job to suspect *everybody*."

And, immediately afterwards, allowing none of those present to recover their composure after that remark whose repercussions were likely to be considerable, he turned towards Arthur Hibbs who, ensconced in an armchair, was observing all this questioning with a perfectly detached, nonchalant air.

"Mr. Hibbs," he said, "I wish to ask you for a very specific piece of information. Where did you spend the evening, and what were you doing at the moment the tragedy occurred?"

Arthur was a young man of about twenty-five years of age, tall, slim, with a perfectly distinguished appearance, and unquestionably elegant. His face didn't reflect any concealed thoughts, and the regularity of his features lent him such an open and frank expression that he was liked by all who saw him, from the very outset.

A fleeting smile played about his lips, yet his eyes blinked several times as he replied: "What? Where was I? But...in my bedroom! I was there for the whole evening; I read, or rather *reread*, a volume by Oscar Wilde: its title is *The Picture of Dorian Gray*, since you require such precise details."

This didn't seem to make any impression on the investigator who, having noted this answer, went on: "You are aware that Sir Roger Bradford died about half an hour ago. Can you tell me why you arrived at his home a quarter of an hour after his death?"

Arthur Hibbs shrugged his shoulders and replied, somewhat disdainfully: "If he died half an hour ago, how come *you* are already here? Might you, by any chance, have been present when Sir Roger was killed?"

Burke didn't appear at all disturbed or offended by the sharp, sarcastic reply that had been made to him, and nobody would think that he bore the slightest resentment towards, or grudge of any description against, the young man.

There remained one further witness to question. But that witness, in truth, could not furnish the detective with any significant information bearing on his investigation. The witness in question was Lucile, the only and much-loved daughter of the victim.

Burke bowed to her.

"Miss," he said, "I deeply respect your grief and will ensure not to question you at any length. Please accept my deepest condolences and my sincerest wishes that time will soon heal your sorrow, and forgive me for all these questions that I'm obliged to ask in your presence, but as you well know, my duty makes it necessary."

Between sobs, she stammered: "I understand, Sir, and please don't postpone or curtail your investigations on my account. I will assist you to whatever extent you may require, and I shall be always ready to be of service to you."

Burke thanked her by a further bow, and then, distancing himself a little from the assembled group, he looked at each of these people who were supplying him with evidence, in turn, and said, in an almost toneless voice, one in which no hint of personal emotion was discernible: "My duty, indeed, was to question each and every one of you, even though the note I found on the dead man's table leaves no doubt as to the cause of this tragedy. My duty now is to reveal the contents of that note to you: Sir Roger committed suicide."

His declaration was greeted with astonishment. Wasn't this really a shocking twist that nobody, quite obviously from their appearance, could have anticipated?

Like all detectives, Burke was probably quite partial to dramatic effect, because, for a few seconds, he allowed himself to savour the surprise and consternation that he had caused; then, searching in his pocket, he took out a piece of paper, which he unfolded and held up in his hand.

"When I arrived here," he said, "I noticed, on Sir Roger's table, a piece of paper that had been conspicuously placed on the blotter. It's only natural that, in the shock immediately following the discovery of the victim's body, nobody noticed this sheet of paper. However, the contents of this note are most explicit. Please allow me to read it to you, even though it is addressed specifically to Lady Lucile."

There was a complete, heavy silence. Burke readjusted his spectacles to allow him to better read the handwritten note, brought the paper close to his nose and read the contents aloud, slowly, and pausing after each word.

> *Lucile,*
> *I have decided, of my own volition, to kill myself; forgive me*
> *for the pain that I'm about to cause you.*

Burke lifted his head from the note. That was all that was contained in the letter, and his piercing eyes once more fixed themselves on the assembled witnesses, waiting to observe their reactions.

Lucile had stood up from her seat.

Her grief seemed to have suddenly vanished and her eyes burned feverishly bright, while her fingers tore her handkerchief to shreds; she then vehemently declared: "That is simply not possible, Mr. Burke; my father had no reason to commit suicide."

And Sir James added, in support of her rebellious contradiction of the letter's words: "I believe Lucile to be right," he stated decisively. "Are you really sure that you aren't mistaken, Mr. Burke? This declaration of an intention to commit suicide doesn't, in my opinion, resolve the strange mystery surrounding this tragedy. I urge you not to cease your enquiry by coming to a conclusion that may be false; please continue with your investigation."

The detective approached Williams, handed the unfolded piece of paper to him, and asked him the straightforward question: "Williams, do you recognize your master's handwriting on this note?"

The butler lowered his head, took the paper in his slightly-trembling hands, studied it at length and then gave it back to the detective, murmuring: "Alas! This is indeed my unfortunate master's handwriting. I have no doubt that it was he himself who wrote this letter."

Burke looked at the assembled family members and seemed to bask in a triumphant glory that bore no trace of humility: "So," he declared, "there you have it!"

None of the appalled witnesses uttered a single word, but Sir James and Lucile were shaking their heads, while Hibbs, his hands folded, seemed to be attentively studying the opposite wall. Was he displaying a complete lack of interest in these proceedings? Or did he feel resentment towards the detective who had been so insultingly inquisitive towards him?

"Therefore," Burke went on, "my report to the authorities will conclude that this was a suicide, so I really think that, under the circumstances, none of you will be bothered any further by the police."

II

For the Past Five Years…

SIR ROGER BRADFORD'S death had, in sum, remained a mystery. The official enquiry, basing itself on Detective Burke's perfectly clear report, had concluded that Sir Roger's death was caused by suicide and the police had had no further involvement in the case. It could indeed be said that, five years after his death, nobody gave any further thought to Sir Roger, apart from a few friends who had known him and his family personally.

Lucile was probably the only person who still moved heaven and earth in an attempt to prove that her father had not at all committed suicide.

She was living in Sir James' house, in the company of Sir James himself, and Arthur Hibbs.

Alas! Sir Roger's house had well and truly undergone a dramatic transformation since those happy days when it had been full of life and bustle.

Even though the residence had been advertised, for sale or rent, by means of publicly affixed notices and small ads in the press, nobody had wanted to live in it. And, in the space of five years, deprived as it was of all upkeep, it had become the gloomiest of abandoned houses.

Naturally, people began to say that it was "haunted".

In England, every time a mysterious death shakes up the usual, deceptive harmony of understandable, natural events, people's minds turn the mysterious place of occurrence of that demise into a ghostly lair.

In the desolate grounds of the mansion, grass and weeds grew uncontrollably; trees that were now free of the attention of billhooks and pruning shears randomly strewed their parasitic offshoots all round them; and, in the corners of irreparably closed windows, bats would hang during the day, and, in the first hours of darkness, would fly round that dwelling in which there was nobody to contest their squatters' rights.

The interior of the dwelling house was even more desolate and forbidding.

Sir Roger's fortune had never been considerable; and, during his lifetime, he must have allowed many parts of his house to fall into disuse and disrepair, confining himself to maintaining only those rooms that were actually lived in.

In the aftermath of his demise, nature, whose powers of disintegration are commonly exercised, had done its best to reduce to naught, all of that which had once adorned and decorated the house of a human being.

Many people living in the neighbourhood, when passing by that house on winter nights, would only risk a hasty sidelong glance at it and then hurry away towards less spine-chilling quarters.

It was even claimed – and certain folk swore that it wasn't at all an optical illusion – that lights had been seen behind the first-floor windows.

When all these rumours were reported to Sir James' household, Roger Bradford's cousin would shrug his shoulders with a melancholy air, and state categorically that he didn't believe in such nonsense.

As for Arthur Hibbs, he appeared much more interested in the above reported sightings, and would often ask probing questions that made the eager tellers of these ghostly tales feel quite awkward.

He especially wished to know if there were still bats to be seen there. Did he have some particular affection for bats, then?

It should be pointed out that Arthur Hibbs was the person for whom Lucile had the strongest preference and friendship.

She certainly had a lot of affection for Sir James too, but the latter seemed so far removed from practical worldly concerns, his dreamy spirit carrying him so often beyond the real limits of life, that the young woman didn't derive much comfort from their conversations. And it was almost as if Sir James himself sought to avoid her on certain occasions and was afraid of being alone with her.

Sir James' kitchen was a kingdom ruled with an iron fist by Betty, the cook, and Harris, the handyman, gardener, cleaner and stove-keeper.

Williams, who had been the butler of the late Roger Bradford, had found refuge at Sir James' house, but he still seemed to consider that dwelling as merely a temporary accommodation; and never, up to now, had he appeared to think that he had taken up permanent residence there.

At times he could be seen – mainly in the early evening – walking in the grounds and inspecting, through a permanently-closed gate, the garden of his former master's house. Who knows what secret regrets he had left behind in that place…?

Anytime that anyone spoke to him about Sir Roger, he would avoid answering, and would change the subject as quickly as possible.

Lucile was convinced that Williams knew more than he was letting on about her father's death; and, one day, she had confided in Arthur about this suspicion of hers.

But that young man had gently reassured and calmed her, asking her not to dwell any further on those things that were needlessly torturing her mind.

"Your father is dead, Lucile," he had said. "Let him rest in peace; unfortunately, there's nothing to prove that he didn't deliberately take his own life. Believe me, life can still be happy for you."

So then she found solace with the passing of time, despite not being able to forget.

One day, however, there was an almighty commotion in the kitchen. It was a few weeks after Christmas, at that time of year when the whole of England seems to slumber and do penance.

Sir James, Arthur and Lucile, who were in the living room on the first floor, silently reading various books while waiting for the bell announcing dinner to be rung, suddenly heard raised voices that caused them to look up from their respective volumes; and they looked at each other, wondering what on earth could be upsetting the silent peace of that austere dwelling.

Sir James was the first to react, dragged abruptly as he was from his usual state of reverie.

"What's going on," he said, "is somebody else being murdered?"

There were certain words that were not to be uttered in that household, and Sir James' careless allusion to previous tragedy had an extreme effect on Lucile, who shuddered.

"Oh!" she said, "how can you say such a thing, Uncle? I recognize that madwoman Betty's voice, and…hold on a moment, I'm sure we're just about to find out what it's all about, because I can hear footsteps on the stairs."

Indeed, the sound of people galloping up the stairs now resounded throughout the echo-filled old house.

Lucile stood up to open the door and Betty rushed into the room, followed at some distance by Harris, who seemed very ill at ease, and who was awkwardly turning round in his hands an apron that he'd picked up somewhere and which clearly didn't belong to him, as it had a lace trimming and feminine stitching.

"Well, Betty, what on earth is the matter? Well?"

This was all Lucile could manage to say; Betty's expression was so terrified that Lucile felt somewhat disturbed by it, and betrayed her disquiet by an excessive flush in her cheeks.

"Miss!" exclaimed Betty, "there are ghosts in the house next door!"

Lucile was just about to cry out: "What! Only that?" but she checked herself.

Betty was, in fact, a woman who saw ghosts everywhere.

She was a plump woman in rude good health, but who was perpetually panic-stricken and blamed her usual mistakes on ghosts and phantoms of every description.

She was an avid reader of novels of the supernatural, and generally blamed the most innocent of sounds on the evil acts of spectres and phantoms.

She moaned. "Sir James, Miss Lucile! Don't make fun of me. This time I really *have* seen ghosts, and I'm not the only one: Harris has seen them too..."

Even though Betty's statements could, to some extent, be taken with a grain of salt, Harris' accounts of what he had witnessed were worthy of being accorded absolute credence, as much as if they'd been issued with the seal of the Bank of England.

Harris was a sturdy man, physically and psychologically robust, and the least likely to be influenced by the wanderings of an unbalanced mind.

He was a man from rural Wales, who had come to London in order to seek his fortune and conquer the world and, had he not been betimes under the thrall of whiskey, he could have been counted on as a strictly neutral and reliable witness in all of life's circumstances. It was therefore to him that Sir James now spoke: "What on earth does this mean, Harris; you saw ghosts?"

Harris opened his mouth, closed it again, and looking at his master straight in the eye, responded with certainty, clarity and firmness, and even put out his hand as if to swear an oath on it: "Yes, Sir, I saw them!"

"And where was this?"

"In the house next door!"

"What did they look like?"

This time, the handyman was stopped short, and looked to Betty. He didn't seem to have a very clear idea of what type of ghost he'd seen, and the cook, coming to his rescue, spoke garrulously: "You can see now that I'm not lying to you," said she, "for Harris says exactly the same as I do, and Harris has no fear of anything; everybody knows that!"

And she was speaking so quickly that her words were practically indecipherable.

"He backs up what I've said, and, this time, you'll have to believe me, yes, you'll really have to. I would prefer to leave this house if anybody were to doubt what I can swear to in the name of the Lord!"

"Calm yourself, Betty," replied Lucile, "I must admit that I don't believe that ghosts can be seen so easily, and you must certainly have made a mistake, but if you will only tell us your story calmly, we'll be quite happy to listen to it."

"So here's what happened, not more than ten minutes ago, and I swear I'm not telling a word of a lie. I was coming back with Harris in the pony and trap. He'd brought me to Maida Vale to go shopping for some pear tree plants..."

"To put on the trellis at the back of the garden," declared Harris, "since the previous ones all perished in the bitterly cold weather."

"Let her continue," said Sir James, "even if she's talking nonsense."

Betty sighed; it was truly very difficult for her to make herself heard or to have the slightest credence placed in her stories.

"At the end of the day," she went on, "I really must tell you what's going on. So we were coming back, Harris and I, in the cart, and he was kind enough to tell me that..."

"To tell her that her company was most pleasant," confirmed Harris, nodding his head.

"Exactly," Betty went on, "that's what he told me, and I was remarking to him that I too was very happy to be acquainted with him, because he's a very polite fellow, from a good family. So, we'd arrived in front of Sir Roger's house, and he'd stopped the horse for a moment, to...to..."

"To kiss her," Harris finished her sentence, having seen that the cook couldn't make up her mind to do so.

Sir James started in his chair. "What?" he asked, "Harris wanted to kiss the horse?"

Betty blushed. "No, it wasn't the horse whom he wanted to kiss, it was *me*, but, naturally, I wouldn't let him, and I bent my head to one side to avoid his lips, and of course, as I was doing that, I turned my eyes in the direction of the late Sir Roger's house. And what did I see at that very moment but a gleam of light gliding along the first floor, passing alongside all the windows. I screamed, and Harris cried: 'What's the matter with you, then, my pretty little Betty, have I done you a mischief?' So I told him to look at the windows; he looked too, and…he saw the lights!"

Betty stopped. Lucile turned toward Harris, who seemed more uncomfortable than ever, and gave him a questioning look. Upon which the Welshman authoritatively confirmed Betty's words.

"As far as lights are concerned," he said hoarsely, "I saw lights, they were lights that you might describe as" - here he paused to find the right word – "electric, they were going out and coming on again as though someone were switching them on and off; so I said to myself 'Those are lights that are certainly not ordinary lights in a house where nobody is living.' Because I had thought at first that perhaps it was people who were looking for matches, but looking for matches in a house where nobody has been living for the last five years, that's something you rarely see, I said to myself, and so, then…"

He stopped.

"Go on, keep going," Betty encouraged him, "tell them what you saw after that, you know quite well that you haven't yet told them the whole story."

"After that," Harris went on, "I was still looking, of course, and I saw what looked like two shadows coming out of the house and walking off through the garden arm in arm!"

Sir James asked: "How could you have seen two shadows, since it was pitch dark?"

"Begging your leave, Sir," Harris respectfully replied, "I saw those shadows because the moon was behind them, and the moonlight was shining on the wall."

Arthur Hibbs himself seemed disturbed by this account and looked at the two servants in turn, trying to make up his mind about their story.

"All that is quite curious and worrisome," he said, "and it's worth looking into. Sir James, will you be so kind as to now allow Betty and Harris to take their leave, with our thanks?"

Sir James thus allowed the cook and the Welshman to take their leave of the living room; they both went back downstairs to the kitchen, continuing to talk about the supernatural apparition, on which no conclusion had been reached.

Lucile, as soon as the two servants were out of earshot, said to Sir James: "I have to admit that I find all this slightly worrying, even though Betty seems quite mad to me and Harris quite stupid; we're going to need someone else's account of this matter." And, as though a new idea had suddenly come into her mind: "What about asking Williams?"

"Why not? Williams is a rational man, a careful thinker who may be useful to us."

To tell the truth, Williams was quite slow in answering the summons to the living room, but he finally appeared, looking more prim and proper than ever, and still as cold and undemonstrative as always.

"Williams," said Sir James, "Betty and Harris are positive that they've seen people in the house next door – people and lights; do you know anything about this?"

Williams hesitated; he looked at Lucile and didn't speak until that young woman had given him permission to do so by a slight movement of her hand. Williams still considered Lady Lucile to be his only superior and employer.

"It is quite possible," he stated in his calm voice, "that the cook and that other fellow" - Williams never referred to Harris by anything other than that expression, as he didn't have much regard for that character who, in his opinion, lacked decorum - "saw people in Sir Roger's house; I have to admit that I've already noticed something unusual in there."

"Do you believe that the house is haunted?" asked Arthur.

Williams shook his head. "I've always heard it said," he replied, "that ghosts didn't make any noise, but this evening, from my bedroom, I heard something that intrigued me."

"What did you hear?" asked Sir James.

The reply was rather vague. "Noises…that's all I can say, noises that I could only describe as…well, it was as if somebody was walking around and moving the furniture."

There followed a silence in the living room. Arthur quickly broke it: "So we must find out what's behind all this," he said.

But just at the very moment when they were probably going to come up with a plan of action, the telephone rang, and Sir James went to answer it.

He lifted up the receiver, and Lucile and Arthur could see that, according as his unseen correspondent spoke on, an obvious joy and relief illuminated the face of the master of the house. They waited, finding the conversation to be too long for their liking.

Finally, Sir James hung up.

"That was the solicitor phoning me," he explained. "He's just informed me that Sir Roger's house has at last been let. I'm no longer astonished that Harris and Betty saw lights in there and that Williams heard noises coming from inside the house. The new tenants visited the premises this very day, after nightfall."

Lucile breathed a sigh of relief.

"So that explains it," she said.

And then she added, after a moment's reflection:

"But who on earth could have taken out a lease on a house like that, given the state it's in? It's absolutely unfit for human habitation!"

Sir Roger's Tenants

IT WAS TIME TO FACE facts: those leaseholders who had taken a liking to the haunted house were no ordinary tenants.

The story of the lease, as recounted by the solicitor, sent shivers down the spine of all who heard it.

He had recently received, in his office, a man who claimed to be a professor, but who didn't specify exactly what subjects he lectured in, and who was accompanied by a young woman who was, admittedly, exceedingly beautiful, but whose beauty was unusual, so out of the ordinary that the solicitor was quite at a loss to find words that would have been adequate to describe it.

"She was like a dead woman who had just recently emerged from her tomb…"

And he lowered his voice to a mere whisper, as though he were fearful of suddenly seeing the spectral apparition of that woman appear before his eyes.

The professor (we are still referring to the solicitor's description of him) was a man of about sixty, hunchbacked, stooped, and dressed in a dark Inverness cape to which he seemed to be surgically attached, so perpetually did he wear it, not even taking it off in the office.

"The thing that struck me most forcibly," said the solicitor, "was his strange, silent, sarcastic little laugh. It gave me the impression that this professor found it impossible to ever close his mouth. From his gums, constantly exposed to view, emerged two rows of sparkling teeth that gave his face a ferocious expression. One's eyes were constantly drawn to this bizarre set of teeth. They reminded me of those of some carnivorous beast, always at the ready to cruelly devour its prey."

The solicitor assured Sir James that he had indeed been careful to let the tenant know that, should he accept the lease on the house, the owner wouldn't be obliged to carry out repairs of any description – to which the professor had replied:

"I shan't require any repairs to be carried out; this dwelling-house suits me exactly as it is."

Upon hearing the account of such remarkable selflessness, Sir James declared with amazement that he would never have thought that any human being could possibly live in such a dark and sinister lair.

"No repairs required!" he exclaimed, "but surely he doesn't intend to live in such a wretched hovel in its present state of repair?"

The solicitor didn't know what to say in reply. He simply declared that, in this day and age, some people had such bizarre notions that nothing should come as a surprise to us nowadays.

And away he went, nonetheless feeling quite delighted to have negotiated a successful transaction and to have finally gotten rid of that residence in which he had no confidence whatsoever. No English solicitor likes to possess, in his office, the title deeds to a building reputed to be in thrall to evil spirits. Such a thing was generally prejudicial to their reputation amongst their serious clients, who prefer to see ghosts in the houses of others, rather than in their own.

Sir James remained silent on the matter of this conversation with the solicitor, and made little comment on the transaction. In response to Lucile's questioning, he said that he would set about clearing up and finalizing this leasehold transaction; and indeed, over the next two days, he was hardly at home.

In particular, he had insisted that the lease be signed, and the solicitor had interceded with the leaseholder with a view to having these legal formalities completed as quickly as possible, as his client had not turned up at the first appointment that had been arranged.

However, on the second day, the solicitor telephoned and said that he was coming over with the lease.

Well, when Sir James had taken a look at the signature, he jumped with extreme shock.

The solicitor, to whom he gave a questioning look, could only nod his head and reply (being even more agitated than Sir James): "Yes, I noticed it too…and I must admit that it doesn't make any more sense to me than it does to you…"

Sir James wiped the sweat from his brow and, without letting anybody know what he was doing, he proceeded to investigate this matter, making several enquiries that didn't furnish him with satisfactory information at all.

On the third day, he returned home with a countenance that had recovered its serenity, and Lucile, who had been watching his puzzling comings and goings with some concern, had reason to believe that he was bearing good news at last.

She asked: "Is there any new information? Have you finally managed to discover the key to the mystery that surrounds us?"

Though she was anxious and impatient, Sir James managed to reassure her.

"Not as yet," he answered, "it's all extremely complicated, but I'm expecting a caller this evening who's going to help us get to the bottom of all this."

And indeed, in the course of the evening, somebody arrived at the house, just after dinner had been finished, and the caller had his card sent in to Sir James.

This was obviously the visitor whom the owner of the house had been expecting, for, as soon as he held the card in his hand, a smile overspread his face and he handed the card to Lucile and Arthur, who were keeping him company.

The two young people read:

> *Edward C. Burke*
> *Criminologist*
> *Saint-Charles Hotel.*
> *LONDON, S.W.*

Lucile looked up with astonishment.

"Burke!" she exclaimed, "but isn't that the detective who made the official report of suicide five years ago?"

Sir James nodded in confirmation.

"It's one and the same," he said. "Given that it's proving impossible to find out anything, and in view of the surprising facts that I've since discovered, I determined to engage the services of a private detective. I remembered Burke, and went to see him this very afternoon..."

Arthur Hibbs gave a slight sneer and, interrupting Sir James, murmured skeptically:

"Permit me to point out to you, Uncle, that you could have chosen more wisely. My recollection of this Mr. Burke – and remember, I did observe him carrying out his duties at the time of the tragedy – doesn't give me any reason to believe that he's one of the leading lights of the criminal investigations branch of the police. His investigation was patently inadequate and he completely ignored the information that Lucile gave him."

"What do you expect me to do? I just thought that Mr. Burke, who is familiar with our family tragedy, could be more useful to me than anyone else. Perhaps he didn't show great skill when the body was discovered, I grant you that, but I can assure you nonetheless that he still remembers all the details, to this very day. Would you believe, my visit didn't seem to cause him the slightest astonishment? You would almost have thought he was expecting me. And yet, he hasn't been a member of the official police force for the past two years."

"But of what relevance is that?" asked Arthur, wondering how that last part of Sir James' reply could have any significance.

"What is relevant about it," Sir James went on, "is that he now has much more freedom than in the past, to devote to us, and he will give us all his time and attention. He has promised me that he won't give up on this matter before it has been completely resolved. As you see, he has come here immediately and I might as well tell you now that he's going to be our guest here for as long as we need him…or for as long as he needs us."

Lucile remarked: "In that case, it would be as well to let Williams know, so that he can get a bedroom ready for our guest."

"I had thought of that," said Sir James.

And he immediately rang for the butler.

The butler came in and was informed by his master of this new duty expected of him. He was instructed to get the apartments ready for Mr. Burke and to take up his suitcases.

Williams reacted to this instruction with apparent indifference but, as he was leaving the drawing room, Lucile was quite surprised to notice that his hands were trembling, as though he was unable to conceal some real agitation, undoubtedly stirred up at the memory of the past tragedy.

After this, Sir James asked for Mr. Burke to be shown in.

He came in, all smiles and attentions, and Lucile recognized that keen, sharp look that she had observed in the past, under the cover of thick spectacles.

"Well!" he exclaimed, "here you all are, in good health; I'm delighted to see it. Lady Lucile, you have a glowing complexion that is a pleasure to behold. As for you, Mr. Hibbs, your serious expression only serves to make your natural distinction even more pleasant to observe. I'm absolutely delighted to see you all again, and I look forward to the time we're going to spend together."

He seemed perfectly at ease and didn't seem to think he had been invited to come to this house for anything other than his own personal enjoyment.

However, the anxiety of those around him made him quickly realize that it was better to get down to the business at hand, and he asked Sir James to give him a second account of the events that had unfolded since the tragedy, an account of which he had already heard a concise version that afternoon.

And, as Sir James was speaking, leaving nothing out, Burke was observing the faces of the two young people much more attentively than that of the narrator of the events. It was as if he was more interested in their reactions than in the facts themselves.

When Sir James had finished, Burke rubbed his hands and lit a cigar. He appeared increasingly satisfied at the turn that this extraordinary adventure had taken over the years throughout which he had not been involved with it.

"That's fine," he said. "Now, we can begin with the certainty of success. May I ask Lady Lucile and Mr. Hibbs to leave us on our own for a moment, as I wish to speak to Sir James privately."

The two young people went out of the room and Burke, as soon as he was on his own with the master of the house, went directly to the heart of the matter: "Now," he said, "may I ask you to conceal nothing from me, and to tell me everything you didn't dare to say in the presence of your nephew and Sir Roger's daughter?"

Sir James looked at him with newfound and sudden seriousness, and a look of fear, which he didn't bother trying to hide, passed over his face. He lowered his voice.

"The fact is," he said, "that things are even more surprising than you might think. I asked you to come back because I'm convinced that those bizarre people who took out a lease on the Bradford house three days ago are somehow implicated in his death."

The criminologist shook the ash from his cigar into a glass ashtray on the table, and continued, in an unruffled manner: "Yet the fact is that we found his suicide note and revolver beside the body. Are those not proof of suicide – yes or no?"

Sir James shook his head. "Admittedly, yes," he replied hesitantly, "but I have other reasons to be alarmed. For example, look at this; what do you make of this, which I found yesterday in the drawer of my desk?"

He handed the detective a sheet of paper that was none other than the suicide note which Burke had taken from the body five years previously, and the detective now reread it aloud in order to get the words firmly fixed in his mind:

Lucile,

I have decided, of my own volition, to kill myself; forgive me for the pain that I'm about to cause you.

But underneath, in capital letters, a hand that was not that of the deceased man had written the following strange words:

DON'T TRY TO SOLVE THIS MYSTERY; THAT'S THE ADVICE I'M GIVING YOU.

Burke looked up at Sir James in astonishment.

"Now there's a thing!" he exclaimed. "How on earth did anybody manage to get hold of this note? It was locked away in my records, in the middle of the case file, and it's clearly the same document. Look, in the corner, you can still see the number 'eight' that indicates its file reference. That figure was written by me in pencil on the note, five years ago. I recognize it only too well."

Sir James was clearly unable to resolve this question and he simply spread his arms out in disbelief, with an expression of doubt on his lips.

And then, after a sigh that betrayed his anxiety, he added: "That isn't all."

"Ah!" said the detective. "What else are you going to tell me?"

Sir James reached for his portfolio and took out the lease that the solicitor had given him. He handed it over with a trembling hand.

"And here is the lease," he said, "that the solicitor gave to the new tenants of my cousin's house. Look at the signature."

Burke readjusted his glasses, brought the document to his nose and let it fall back on his knees; he seemed to be in the grip of profound disbelief and astonishment.

"Wonderful!" he exclaimed, "this lease is signed 'Roger Bradford'."

"Yes," murmured Sir James. "So has the dead man come back to live in his own house?"

The detective allowed himself a few minutes for reflection and declared – as anybody in his position might similarly have stated – that it was probably just a simple coincidence, that of an identical name, which wasn't inconceivable, since the name "Bradford", though not common, was borne by several families in the British Isles.

But in actual fact, this probably wasn't the sincere expression of his thought, for this explanation visibly lacked fervour and conviction. So he wasn't surprised when Sir James shook his head, replying: "No, Mr. Burke, I'm only too familiar with this signature to make a mistake; it's Roger Bradford's, I'm sure of it. Nothing allows me to doubt that fact; none of the peculiarities of his handwriting are absent from the signature. The vertical flourish is identical; it's unimaginable!"

The detective looked at Sir James and observed, on his features, the progress of his growing agitation.

And at that very moment, the sound of hurrying footsteps resounded in the hallway. The door of the drawing room opened and Lucile appeared.

She was extremely pale and her hand, placed on her chest, struggled to contain her rapidly beating heart. She spoke, and her voice quivered with anxiety. She said, under the spell of a great terror that she couldn't manage to rid her mind of:

"This is terrible! I've just heard a voice calling me from the bottom of the garden, and the tone is exactly the same as my father's voice! I beg you, deliver me from this evil; what on earth is going on here? Are you going to let us go mad without trying to do anything to help us?"

Sir James glanced in Burke's direction. The latter, his cigar held vertically in his right hand, was observing the young woman with curiosity; he stood up and went over to her.

Then, taking her by the hand, he made her sit down, had Betty bring her a glass of water and, soothing her with gentle words, which one mightn't necessarily have expected to hear from the heart of a man like him, he waited a few moments before questioning her.

When she had completely recovered, he urged her to describe, in as much detail as possible, the incident she had just experienced.

"I was in my bedroom," said Lucile, "trying to shut the window, which was proving quite difficult to close. Suddenly, from the bottom of the garden, there came a call that was addressed specifically to me, my name, distinctly uttered: 'Lucile.' I was rooted to the spot, so caught unawares was I by the sound of that voice; and the call immediately came again, even clearer and more distinct: 'Lucile! Come to me.' This time, I could be in no doubt. That was exactly how my father used to speak to me in times gone by when he wanted to tell me something in confidence. Then, I was submerged by terror and quickly shut the window, and came to find you without stopping anywhere else. I can't stand this terrible uncertainty any longer."

She fell silent.

"This is getting serious," murmured the detective. "We must make an immediate search of the premises. Let's see…"

He looked round, and seemed to be searching for somebody.

"Let me see," he went on, "I'll need somebody trustworthy. Sir James, could you ask Mr. Hibbs to come here? I wish to send him to comb the house next door, with some of the servants."

"I'll go and search it myself," offered Sir James, moving forward.

"No – I need you for a search of a different kind."

Then, leaning down and taking Lucile by the hand, he said, gently: "Fear nothing, my child; if there's something threatening your security and peace of mind, I assure you that we will uncover it."

Arthur Hibbs agreed to conduct a search of Sir Roger's house, but without enthusiasm; he didn't like being taken advantage of without first being asked how he felt about it. This was no easy or pleasant task, rendered all the more difficult and disagreeable, moreover, by the fact that the servants – only Williams and Harris were available – showed no signs of great delight on learning that they were to be members of the search party about to set forth on its expedition.

Nonetheless, the three of them set off, after listening to the orders of the former police officer, who instructed them to comb everything, including even the smallest clump of flowers or trees, and to open all of the doors; no stone was to be left unturned in conducting a thorough search.

However, Arthur did raise an objection.

"Haven't you told me that there were tenants in Sir Roger's house? What are we to do if they prevent us from searching the premises? We don't have any authority to replace the official police."

"If you're prevented from searching the house," replied Burke, "that in itself will be a valuable clue for us. It will prove that the current inhabitants aren't keen on being visited. If that happens, just make your excuses and leave."

"Very well," said Arthur, "I'll do what I can, and nothing more."

And off he went, accompanied by Williams and Harris, who walked somewhat reluctantly after him.

Once more, Burke found himself alone with Sir James.

"All this is really disturbing," the detective said, "and the first thing we have to do is to check whether Sir Roger's body is still in its tomb. You and I will attend to that task."

Sir James gave a start.

"What!" he stammered, "surely you're not going to make me follow you to his burial place? Do you really think that Sir Roger..."

"I first believe that which I can see," Burke curtly replied, "and then that which I think, but the crucial thing is, first, to *see*."

This errand was quickly executed for, at that time of night, there were few vehicles or passers-by in the streets, and nobody other than these two men felt any desire to visit the city graveyards.

They reached the cemetery, and Burke instructed the coach driver to stay beside the gates and wait for them.

Sir James counted the sarcophagi, calling out, as he went, the names of those who reposed therein.

"One," he said, "..."this is the coffin of Lady Helena Bradford, Sir Roger's mother. Two...this one belongs to Sir Joseph, Roger's father, and there...'three', that's the very coffin of my unfortunate cousin who..."

He stopped, and Burke, who was listening to and observing him surreptitiously, saw that Sir James' face expressed some unutterable astonishment.

"Well?" he asked. "Your cousin's grave, yes...?"

Sir James took hold of Burke's arm and gripped it forcefully, as if he were experiencing the need to feel the presence of a truly living being beside him.

"This is..." he stuttered, "this is Roger's coffin...yes...but...look closely...the lid has slipped off...It's no longer covering the casket underneath!"

Burke shrugged his shoulders.

"What?" he said, "you mean to tell me *that's* all that's bothering you? I noticed *that* fact, the moment we got to this grave; I merely wished to find out who was buried in this spot; you say it's Sir Roger?"

His companion wiped his brow, which was damp with sweat; he murmured in a flat, toneless voice:

"Yes, it's in this very spot that my cousin was buried. But I could never dare look into the coffin myself..."

The detective was certainly less sensitive to the memory of a dead man who had meant nothing to him, and his profession required him to shield himself against the quite natural anxiety that was evident in his guide's mind.

He approached the coffin, knelt down and began by running his fingers between the casket and its lid, after which he stood up and said: "Sir James, as strange as this may seem to you, I have to tell you that the body is no longer there…"

Sir James' lips trembled but no sound came from his mouth. He was gasping for breath, his eyes were wandering in their sockets and his face was so deathly pale that Burke thought he was about to faint.

So Burke, not wishing to subject him to too severe an ordeal, then suggested: "Let's go, shall we? We know enough for now."

They returned to the house without communicating to each other the different and varied impressions that were swirling about their minds.

Burke probably considered it unnecessary to require his companion to tell nobody of this grim discovery, for he didn't give him any advice on this subject and bound him to no secrecy.

Arthur had returned, having completed his search, and he immediately informed the detective that it had proven fruitless.

He had been able to get into the house and all its rooms without any difficulty, for the good reason that there was nobody there. The only companions of his nocturnal visit had been the bats, fluttering about the dilapidated rooms, and he had found no sign of life therein.

The gardens and the park of the house were deserted, and the clumps of trees and flowers – which had been searched as thoroughly as was possible, despite the thorns and brambles – hadn't revealed anything of interest.

"Perfect!" said Burke, "Moreover, I had suspected as much. We know enough for today, and we shall continue our investigation tomorrow. Mr. Hibbs, it only remains for me to thank you."

IV

Do Vampires Exist?

THE NEW DAY DAWNED dull and misty – an inglorious dawn with nothing of brightness or radiance.

Thick fog clung tenaciously to all visible things, and concealed the comforting aura that, in normal weather conditions, was characteristic of this aristocratic district of London.

However, Burke didn't at all alter the habits that were his on ordinary days. He enjoyed a hearty breakfast, and asked for three further helpings of haddock.

By nine o'clock that morning, nobody had yet come downstairs into the dining room.

Thus, having finished his breakfast, he began to inspect the other rooms of the house.

He began his tour of inspection with the drawing room, of which Arthur Hibbs was, at that early hour, the only occupant.

The young man was reading. After the night he'd just had, he no doubt wished to acquire some specific enlightenment on his state of mind; the book he was reading bore an impressive and rambling title, in accordance with the old-fashioned style. Indeed, its title contained no fewer than seven lines:

The Afterlife
Or
The Mystery of Vampires Unveiled:
An Anthology of Ancient
And
Remarkable Phenomena
London 1703

Arthur hardly bothered to raise his eyes from this tome when Burke came into the room, merely absent-mindedly wishing the detective a good morning.

"Don't put yourself out on my account," said Burke.

This was a completely pointless instruction. Arthur Hibbs didn't even take his feet off the armchair on which he had stretched his legs so as to sit more comfortably. He was reading a passage with great concentration and didn't want to be distracted.

After a few moments, his admiration for that particular section of the book was probably so great that he wished to share it with Burke; and, showing no qualms about interrupting the detective's own reading – Burke had picked up the morning paper, left in the drawing room by Williams – Hibbs enthused:

"It's incredible what you can learn from reading these old authors, and especially the learned alchemists of the sixteenth century. Although, come to think of it, these are things you ought to be already familiar with."

Burke asked, in a simple and unaffected manner, what the passage in question was about, and the young man began to explain it to him, delighted to have the opportunity of sharing his newfound knowledge.

"It's all about vampires; not at all the kinds of vampiric creatures that exist in tropical forests, but actual vampires who are the incarnation of human beings who died with the stain of sin in their souls. To tell you the truth, it was those bats I saw last night that gave me the idea of finding out something about these mysteries – mysteries that this book claims to have unveiled."

"And what does your book have to say about these vampires?" asked Burke, without any visible signs of genuine interest or respect.

"It says," Arthur went on, "that vampires are neither ghosts nor spectres emanating from the kingdom of shadows, but are rather the reincarnation of dead people who temporarily leave their tombs and feed on the blood of the living."

The detective cut him short.

"My God!" he exclaimed, "were you stung by some sleep-inducing creature last night, by any chance? I must admit that, as far as I'm concerned, I have little time for this supernatural mumbo-jumbo, and vampires have never come between me and my night's sleep, nor have they ever given me indigestion."

Impervious to the sarcasm of that remark, the young man continued: "It goes on to say that, if they are seen or caught during daylight hours, vampires sometimes assume the form of bats and then try to get some sleep in the solitude of damned, accursed haunts of the undead."

"Ah! Yes – is that so?" said Burke.

He looked at the young man with mocking, sardonic faux-seriousness and, standing up, went over and unceremoniously closed the book that the latter was reading.

And just as Arthur was about to protest at this rude behaviour (what a nerve that detective had!), Burke once again interrupted him, halting the words that were about to issue from the young man's lips, and said to him: "Might I enquire, Mr. Hibbs, as to the cause of your sudden interest in vampires? I'm sure you aren't under the illusion that I'm about to believe that vampires have had anything to do with the case that currently interests us; are you actually accusing them of killing Sir Roger? Now *that* would be indeed odd."

The young man winced slightly, and, after a brief silence, replied: "I'm not under any illusions whatsoever, and you are free to believe whatever you like. As for me, I find this subject to be a curious one, and worthy of study by a cultured gentleman; that's all."

"And who encouraged you to consult this book?" asked the detective.

Arthur nodded his chin in the direction of the hall. "It was Betty, the cook, who tipped me off about the existence of this book, and she herself it was who showed me the place where it was kept in the library. Personally, I'd never seen it before."

Burke began to laugh. "The fact that Betty may believe in vampires only half-surprises me, but you! Now that's a different kettle of fish!"

"Don't I have the right to believe in them if I so choose?" retorted the young man tetchily.

"Indeed, you have every right," replied the detective in an attempt to cool the young man's annoyance, "but I find it astonishing that you would try to persuade me so passionately to share your beliefs, and try to sidetrack me into little highways and byways that ultimately lead nowhere. So what are you hoping to achieve?"

Arthur stood up. He could sense, in Burke's questioning, intentions that seemed unbefitting. Did the detective suspect him of murder? At that moment, Hibbs seemed on the point of angrily reproaching the detective for his inappropriate perseverance, but he checked himself, though not sufficiently to prevent himself from crying out, in a mocking tone: "Whatever the case may be, Mr. Burke, you cannot but accept that Bradford's tomb was empty!"

"The tomb was empty, yes, that fact is perfectly correct, but could you explain to me, young man, how you came to be informed of that state of affairs?"

Arthur Hibbs had probably expected a question of that nature, and he replied with apparently complete truthfulness: "Because last night, quite simply, I went to see Sir James in his room, and he told me what the two of you had gone to check at the cemetery. I presume it's quite natural for an uncle to confide in his nephew?"

The merest hint of a smile played about Burke's lips.

He had been in a position to perceive the razor sharp intellect of this young man, and he good-humouredly reminded him at that moment of the sentence he, Hibbs, had uttered when, five years previously, Burke had expressed surprise at the fact that the young man had been in his room at the moment of Sir Roger's demise.

"Your answer to me was," he said: ""If he died not more than half an hour ago, how come you've got here so quickly?' It was a very good point, Mr Hibbs, and I have to admit that, at the time, you really put me on the spot."

Just then, Sir James came into the room, and his presence brought great relief to Arthur, who bustled and fussed about his uncle, anxiously inquiring as to whether he had had a good night's sleep. His excessive concern was even noticed by the uncle, who wasn't accustomed to such excessive considerateness and attentiveness on the part of his nephew.

It was obvious that Sir James hadn't slept well; this could be seen from the purple-hued shadows under his eyes, his haggard, drawn features and his general air of weariness.

He turned towards the detective with a worried look, and asked: "Have you found out anything new?"

Burke had no specific new information to impart, and he probably didn't like being in this position, as his inability to report anything new placed him in a situation of inferiority vis-à-vis those employing him.

Thus, following their fruitless efforts of the night before, Sir James began to speak of this and that, and as he happened to notice, at that moment, the book Arthur was reading, the conversation turned to the heinous deeds of vampires; upon which was made, in relation to that book, a remarkable observation: the detective had said: "Mr. Hibbs was just reading with great interest, that book, which he found in your library yesterday..."

Sir James replied that, to his knowledge, he didn't have any books about vampires in his collection. He had never taken any interest in the occult, and didn't lose any sleep over the spectres of the dead.

Burke then took mischievous pleasure in causing a difference of opinion between uncle and nephew on matters supernatural, and for the next quarter of an hour, observed the discussion that ensued on this subject between the two men.

Then, asking the two gentlemen to remain in the drawing room, he went himself to fetch Betty, who came back with him, and waited, somewhat flustered by so much honour, to find out what was wanted of her.

Burke simply wanted to know whether anything out of the ordinary had occurred during the night in Lucile's bedroom.

"*I* can't say for sure what I saw was extraordinary, but I did see *something*," she said.

"Ah!" said the detective, "now we're getting somewhere! Tell us what you saw, my good woman."

And, with kindness and gentleness, he set about "hearing Betty's confession," as she was clearly reluctant to tell her story. Nevertheless, the criminologist went to such pains to be friendly and courteous towards her that she finally allowed herself to be persuaded to tell all, her reservations having been overcome in the end.

"I don't know what time it was," she said, "when I saw, on the other side of the window – outside, that is – an unusual shape that seemed to be looking into the bedroom from just outside the window pane."

"What did this shape look like?" asked Burke.

Betty strove to make her description as clear as possible.

"Well…a shape…not exactly like that of a normal man, but an animal with wings. He wasn't standing on the windowsill…no, he seemed to be attached to the pane of glass, like…like a bat, and I saw his face, and it was terrible to behold! Alarming, Sir, there's no other word for it, and you would feel as frightened as me if you had seen it for yourself. Believe it or not, the creature had a man's face, white as the moon, and it was laughing all the time; that's what I noticed immediately; it was laughing. Its enormous mouth and white teeth looked as though they wanted to devour us!"

"Ah!" said Burke. Then, speaking to Sir James, he asked: "Doesn't that laugh remind you of anything?"

"Yes," murmured the master of the house. "When the solicitor spoke to me about the tenant who had rented the house, he was emphatic about that silent and constant laugh that had struck him so forcibly."

Burke nodded his head in agreement, and, returning to his questioning of the cook, he wanted to know why she hadn't reported this incident immediately.

The explanation she offered was a plausible one.

"I was afraid of being laughed at," she said. "I'm well aware that when you talk about vampires around here, people think badly of you, and I've already been given a hard time about it."

Burke calmed her down with his hand, tapping her on the shoulder like a groom soothing a nervous horse.

"Leave the ghosts to us, my good woman; we'll deal with them. Go back to your kitchen and cook us a really hearty lunch; I'm absolutely ravenous." And that was truly unbelievable, coming from a man who had already eaten enough, at breakfast, to feed four people; but Mr. Burke was a man who never had any intention of fasting.

Before dismissing Betty, and at the very moment that she was crossing the threshold of the drawing room door, relieved and assured, he asked her one final question.

"Betty, you didn't happen to hear Sir Roger's voice during the night, did you?"

She shivered and replied briefly: "The deceased gentleman's voice? No, Sir."

He then asked the young man to leave him alone with Sir James so that they could talk privately.

"The time has come to admit to you," he said, "that I don't have much trust in your nephew or your maid."

Sir James interrupted him. "What are you going to say against my nephew, Mr Burke; why are you so fixated on him? What do you think he's done wrong?"

"It's nothing I can quite put my finger on," replied the detective, hesitatingly. "I must simply say that he's trying to steer me into a certain line of inquiry; and it makes me uneasy, given that he's such a well-balanced man."

"You mean…vampires?" asked Sir James.

"Precisely: vampires. Oh! He does it very subtly, and nothing of what he says could surprise a man who isn't in the habit of reading hidden meanings into what people say to him."

"But how can you see any connection between my nephew's arguments and Betty's chatter?" asked Sir James, with assurance. "The cook has only been in my employment for two years; she knew nothing about my cousin's death; she has never heard his voice and doesn't know what went on here. She believes that it was suicide. It's not the first time she's spoken about vampires. She has already created panic in the household on two or three occasions with conversations like that. So why should a subject that had been of no importance in the past, suddenly seem so significant now?"

Mr. Burke didn't know everything as yet, and he honestly admitted it.

"Each hurdle must be overcome one at a time," he said, "and we would be wasting our time if we tried to surmount them all, all at once."

"I'm beginning to uncover, in this case," he went on, stressing each of his words, "some exceptionally serious facts."

And, from the seat he was then occupying, Sir James replied: "Don't you think that the first thing we should do is call the police and have them come into both this house and the Bradford house so they can capture whoever they may find in there?"

But Burke replied categorically, and with a sort of repressed rage: "I don't need the police! We will deal with this case *ourselves*, and if you instruct anyone outside of this house to conduct a search, I will immediately withdraw my services."

His tone of voice, which brooked no disagreement, had the desired impact on the master of the house, who didn't dare say anything further.

V

The Investigation Continues

LUCILE AND ARTHUR spent almost the entire afternoon in each other's company.

Certainly, Lucile appeared to place great trust in Arthur, but since hearing her father's voice, she was in an unsurprisingly nervous state. She avoided everybody and the slightest noise made her jump.

Arthur regarded her reactions as nonsense, but was careful not to express this opinion of his, and affectionately strove to reassure the young woman. She had nothing to fear because everybody – he most of all – was thinking only of her protection.

"I'm happy," he said to her, "that you should turn to me at this time of danger; that is proof of your deep trust in me, Lucile, and I must admit to you that, at the moment, I too have serious reasons to be worried."

Lucile looked at him, astonished at the change that had occurred in the young man's tone of voice.

"Worried; why then, Arthur, might you be worried? And worried for whom?"

He hesitated a moment, then, undoubtedly resolving to reveal everything that he had on his mind and in his heart, he slowly declared: "I'm just about certain that Burke suspects me."

Unable to understand, she stepped away from him, joining her hands. "Suspects you! Arthur, what a preposterous idea! How on earth can you think that of Mr. Burke; he's being so nice to us all?"

Arthur shook his head. He realized that his words were not believed, and, somewhat testily, he continued: "The bottom line is that this Burke whom you're defending, is a complete stranger to all of us."

"He was part of His Majesty's police for a long time," said Lucile: "that in itself ought to be a sufficient character testimonial, I should have thought."

Arthur sharply retorted: "But he's no longer part of the police force. Isn't that quite surprising? You'll probably tell me that he had reached retirement age, but then why has he continued to exercise his profession on a private, self-employed basis? I've been making discreet enquiries, I'll have you know. Oh! Obviously, I don't know much; however, I can tell you that Burke was *forced* to resign. It's said in the police stations that it was because of his unorthodox methods, which weren't at all in accordance with those permitted by law. They say he used to go too far when he was trying to extract confessions from suspects, but despite persistent enquiries I haven't been able to find out what exactly his methods consisted of. The one thing that's certain is that his resignation was forced upon him, and under threat of being struck off the official register of existing and former police officers. Don't you find that disturbing?"

Lucile didn't know how to respond. Up to now, she had trusted her friend Arthur as much as she trusted Burke and yet, at this moment, doubt was beginning to creep into her mind.

The whole affair was weighing too heavily on her, for her to be able to reach a definite judgement. Not wishing to hear any more about this, and perhaps feeling that her nerves were on the point of being too roughly shaken, she coolly left the young man and went back to her room to think in solitude.

Furthermore, nothing out of the ordinary took place in the course of that day.

Burke spent his evening questioning Williams, but he was careful not to ask anybody else to witness this interrogation.

It was in the detective's room that this questioning took place and, on exiting the room, Williams seemed so dumbfounded that it was only when Sir James had asked him a third time for a glass of water that he obeyed his master's call.

It was noticed in the kitchen that Williams "seemed distracted". Harris even joked with him rather insensitively. "By Jove!" said he to the butler, who wasn't responding to his provocation, "you look very worried this evening, old fellow; it's almost as if you were about to be arrested and were already in handcuffs!"

Williams reacted badly to this flash of wit. "That's enough!" he exclaimed, "and if people have only such unpleasant and offensive remarks to make to me, I'd prefer to eat alone or even not eat at all!"

And, leaving the servants' hall, he went to his room and wasn't seen again for the rest of the evening.

"Maybe he's writing to his lawyer," said Harris, which was what he was actually thinking.

But nobody could make him any the wiser on that point, for Williams had locked himself away in his room, doubly bolting the door.

In the drawing room, conversation was desultory, and once again, the detective and his investigations were the main topic of discussion. Towards ten p.m., the detective himself was the first to stifle a yawn, and, jokingly, he said to Arthur: "I've got an idea, Mr. Hibbs. What would you say if I were to ask you to allow me to sleep in your room tonight?"

The young man's retort was curt. "I don't suppose, Mr. Burke, that anybody has any intention of getting any sleep tonight. I imagine that we all have other things to occupy our minds. What's more, I have no desire to let you take up half my bedroom; firstly because I have only one bed, and secondly because I have always slept alone."

"What of it!" persisted the detective, "You do have a settee that I could stretch out on; I'm easy to please."

"You would find it most uncomfortable," said Arthur.

"Oh well!" the detective said, "let's not say another word about it, even though it would have been a great pleasure for me, I assure you. I've seen your settee and it's extremely comfortable…"

He stopped for a second, his sentence left unfinished, his brow furrowed.

"It's a double settee, if I'm not mistaken, which you possess in your room. When you lift it up at the bottom, you find a chest where you lock away your books…your books and your personal papers, of course."

The young man stood up with irritation and, making no attempt to mask his anger, retorted: "I don't allow anybody, Mr. Burke, to search my room in my absence. Even accused parties have the right to defend themselves as they wish and to be present at any and all searches or other enquiries in their homes. Even so, I'm not yet accused of anything, I imagine? Therefore, please be kind enough to let me know in advance when you wish to indulge in your little playacting; I'll be there, and we shall be able to delight in it together."

He immediately left the room and Burke began to laugh somewhat awkwardly and forcedly, perhaps to hide his embarrassment. "I didn't think I'd offend him," he said, "I said all that completely innocently, but he's a really touchy character. I wonder whether there's something worrying him…"

That was just about all that was said that evening in the drawing room and, less than a quarter of an hour later, the owners and guest of the house, retiring one after the other, made their way to their rooms.

Sir James had sunk into sleep the moment he had lain down. His sleep had been troubled by nightmares, but it wasn't until almost two o'clock in the morning that he woke up, feeling a hand shaking him.

He awoke instantly after a start had caused him to sit up straight in his bed. Seeing the face of the person who'd awakened him, a relieved though strained smile replaced his terrified expression.

"Oh! It's you, Burke," he said.

The detective, his eyes turned towards the door, signalled to him to get up. "Come with me," he said, "and let's try not to make a racket; there's something I need to show you, but it's for your eyes only."

All of these successive events, which rained down in their turn on Sir James' somewhat dazed brain, hardly allowed him any time to recover; and it was obvious that, ever since he had asked Burke to conduct this investigation, he had experienced a certain confusion in all his faculties.

In vain had the detective tried to make him recall the events that had occurred five years previously. Each time, he came up against memory blanks that might appear unbelievable; thus it was that Sir James could no longer recall exactly at what time of the evening he had discovered his cousin's body, and it was just about impossible to find out from him whether or not he had heard the gunshot.

That might all have appeared astonishing to the detective, had he not remembered Sir James' particularly inconsistent character. In the normal course of events, one could never be sure if he had heard the entirety of the conversations that were made to him. He was always dreaming and thinking of other things.

It was said that he had no memory to speak of and was extremely absent-minded. That must have been indeed true, for even during the first two days that Burke had spent in the house, the master of the dwelling had once lost his watch, and twice his bunch of keys.

"Where are we going?" Sir James now asked.

They went downstairs, taking care not to make the slightest sound that might wake up the household and give the alarm, and arrived in the small park bordering the gardens of the mansion that had formerly been home to Sir Roger.

"It's really cold," remarked Sir James, shivering.

"You ought to have brought your overcoat," the detective pointed out; "Didn't it occur to you that we're no longer in the middle of spring?"

By the light of his electric pocket lamp, Burke could see that his companion's face was deathly pale, his lips trembling.

They walked in single file along the boundary wall separating the two properties, and thereby arrived at the little door that served as a passageway between the two gardens.

"There's no point in going through that door," said the detective; "the creaking would give us away if someone happened to be watching the garden and spying on us. It'll be enough for our purposes just now to look through the railing. Go up to the metal bars and look at what's happening right in front of you, toward the right."

As though attracted by some all-powerful force, Sir James leaned forward, clutching the bars tightly, and looked in the direction indicated by the detective.

And so it was that he froze in horror and disbelief. Burke no longer needed to give him the slightest additional instruction.

At the end of a walkway, in a sort of circular clump of elm trees whose branches had grown level with the ground and that swept over the lawn, he caught sight of the outline of a man who, standing with his hands behind his back, his shoulders slightly stooped, was looking at the house.

Sir James recoiled in horror as though he wished to escape from this vision, and, looking sideways at the detective, stammered: "It's…Roger!… My cousin…but how can this be?…"

"Yes," murmured the detective. "It's Sir Roger; I knew it…He's been standing there for about an hour and it was precisely himself whom I wished to show you, so that there may be two of us who are sure we've seen the same thing."

So this was no illusory apparition, since two clear-minded, lucid observers had – first successively, then together – witnessed the staggering fact.

Normally, ghosts never appear to two different people at the same time, save in certain cases, albeit very rare, of collective hallucination.

Thus there could be no doubt: the man walking in the garden really was Sir Roger, or, at least, he had all the human and physical appearance of that gentleman.

"You knew him better than I did," said Burke, "therefore, can you tell me for certain that it really is him?"

"It's him, it really is him…or else it's nothing but a terrible nightmare!"

Burke didn't want to subject his companion's nerves to too severe an ordeal, as the latter was showing all the signs of imminent convulsions. Burke took his companion's arm in a friendly way and led him back to the house, talking to him reassuringly all the while and even striving, one might say, to erase the troubling vision he had just witnessed.

It was only when they were back in the house, and the warmth and light had partly dissipated the agitation caused by the vision glimpsed in the garden, that Sir James recovered his composure and alertness and replied: "I must admit that I don't understand anything about this resurrection, if indeed it is such; I understand absolutely nothing about it; my cousin had no reason to disappear and fake his death; all his affairs were in order and completely above board."

"My dear Sir, we are no longer faced with a dilemma and the situation is extremely clear. Since it is indeed Sir Roger whom we saw in the garden – you've made a positive identification of him – we must accept the fact that he's still alive. I forbid dead men to walk about in my presence! And, believe me, Sir James, it's easier to get a living person to talk than a dead one. Tomorrow, if you don't see any problem with my proposition, and if you've rested sufficiently, we will look for your cousin and we shan't abandon our investigations until we've found and interviewed him. Once we have him in our hands, both of us, it'll be the devil of a thing if we don't manage to force him to admit the motive behind this macabre joke of his…What is it?"

His question was caused by the signs of refusal that Sir James was exhibiting in the face of these sensible propositions.

"No," he replied, in a hoarse voice, "no; don't count on me, Mr. Burke, to help you in your search. You obviously can't see how overwhelmed I am by the shock of all this. It would be cruel of you to force me to help you with such an interview. Look for Sir Roger by yourself, I beg of you; as for me, this case is becoming so horrifyingly mysterious and threatening, by its unfathomable aspects, that I'm wondering if I even have the strength to remain here."

And he went on to say that he was considering leaving to stay in the Bradford ancestral home deep in the heart of Cornwall, but Burke wouldn't hear of this escape, or of what, in fact, amounted to a desertion.

He declared that Sir James' presence was essential, but that he'd do his best to spare him the mental torture that, very logically, was putting his heart and nerves in such an abominable state.

VI

The Next Day...

THAT MORNING, Burke had once again gorged himself on toast with orange marmalade, as well as bacon and eggs. He had managed to drink, all on his own, a teapot that normally sufficed for three people; and he was now feeling so happy that he was humming a variety-show tune, not seeming to notice that atmosphere of dread which surrounded him and which engulfed, so to speak, every nook and cranny of the mansion and all its inhabitants.

At nine o'clock that morning, nobody had yet come downstairs. Burke had an unfortunate habit of rising much earlier than everybody else. So it was that he waited another half-hour before sending word to Lucile that he needed to speak to her.

The detective – in accordance with his usual manner towards Lucile – was affable and respectful. In his eyes, however, one could read something more tender and affectionate than was ordinarily the case. In the presence of the young woman, he abandoned his abrupt air of authority and his habitual sarcasm.

"Miss," he said, as soon as they were at the edge of the lawn and thus about a hundred paces distant from the steps leading up to the manor's entrance, "I must beg your forgiveness for all the anxiety I've caused you up to now and all the sorrow that I'm still going to occasion you, for, alas, we aren't at all yet out of the woods. You are going to need a lot of courage."

The young woman sighed and tears rose to her eyes.

"I am ready to hear all that you have to say," she said, "but I have to admit that I've never felt such distress and confusion since my father's death. Sir, I implore you to tell me what you know; you can see the degree of friendship – I dare to admit it – with which I am at your service."

He bowed his head.

"And that is precisely the reason," he replied, "why I have asked you, this morning, to grant me this private interview. I wish to finally let you know of the certainties that I have been in possession of for the past five years, though I couldn't yet make them known without risking danger. Your father did not kill himself; but the thing that makes this investigation so delicate is that, for the past five years, you have, in all probability, been living with somebody who knows quite a lot about the crime."

She started in terror and brought her hands to her throat.

"My God!" she exclaimed, "you don't mean that – somebody in this house – murdered him?"

But, in response to her very specific question, Burke merely blinked his eyes, a facial tic that unmistakeably signalled to the young woman: "I can't tell you everything yet; you'll have to trust me for a little while longer."

She sighed: "But why must it be so? Why didn't you tell me any of this sooner?"

He led her briskly around the lawn, and they both walked as if they were two close friends busily confiding in each other, although only Burke was speaking. "I ought not to have admitted to you, even today," he said, "what I know about your father's death, and thereby increase the burden of your sorrow, but it pains me too much to see you so unhappy; and for a sensitive nature such as yours, it's better to learn the cruel truth than continue to suffer in doubt. I don't want you to spend this day in a state of anxiety caused by incomprehensible mysteries; and what's more, you may also be able to help ensure that the truth will out. I'm going to ask you to place your complete trust in me…to do exactly, and all, that I tell you, however extraordinary it may appear to you. The one thing you must promise me is to say nothing of all this…to not breathe a word to a living soul…not to a living soul, you understand, even if someone were to beg you or advise you not to trust me."

Walking by the detective's side, she now grasped his hand and clutched it tightly.

"Mr. Burke," she said, "I have great faith in you, absolute trust; I feel you are my friend; indeed, I sensed it five years ago, that day you came to certify my father's tragic death, and great was my despair when I saw that you seemed to believe it was suicide."

And she waited for his questions.

"First of all," the detective began, "how old were you exactly when your father died?"

"Sixteen years and three months," she replied.

"Very well. You must now forgive me for what may seem to be a personally intrusive question: did you have a fiancé at that time?"

She thought for a moment: "To be honest," she said, "I didn't have a fiancé, but I liked Arthur Hibbs very much and I truly believe that since that time, I've always continued to like him. We weren't engaged, of course, and my father knew nothing of this bond."

"Why not?" asked Burke.

"Because," she replied, "my father used to get angry whenever anybody spoke to him about a possible marriage for me; but I've always liked Arthur...Oh! My God! Surely you aren't going to say that I'm mistaken?"

"For the moment, we're not discussing affairs of the heart, my child; we are simply trying to put the facts in context. All right then; let's continue. So you liked Arthur Hibbs; he is your cousin, I believe?"

"A very distant cousin. In actual fact, I don't think we're even related, but as he was adopted by Sir James, I consider him my cousin, but my father didn't trust anybody who paid me any attention. He always considered me too young!"

"Good!" said Burke. "Have you ever noticed that – apart from Mr. Hibbs – anybody else might have been interested in you; I'm still speaking from a romantic point of view, of course?"

"I do seem to recall something, now that you mention it...but it's so vague that I wonder whether it might not be just a false impression...I remember that Sir James once asked me a very odd question. He asked me if I would be willing to accept, as a husband, a man who would bring me wellbeing and security, even if he were of an age that wasn't exactly what I might have expected."

"Ah!" said Burke. Then he continued: "And did you have any notion at that moment that Sir James might have been speaking of himself?"

She responded keenly, with heartfelt sincerity: "Not for one second; I simply suspected that he had someone in mind to put before me for my consideration, some baronet or other from Surrey – a forty-five-year-old man – who used to sometimes come to visit us and who would occasionally stay over for a day or two. But naturally, I didn't attach much importance to Sir James' question for, shortly afterwards, that supposed suitor left the house and abruptly stopped visiting us."

Burke now seemed to abandon this line of questioning and moved on to a different subject.

"What about speaking a little of Williams?" he cried, almost cheerfully. "That good man has known you since you were very young, if I'm not mistaken."

"He was in service in this house when I was born; I've known him my whole life."

"I thought as much. How has he treated you over the years?"

"He has always been extremely respectful."

"And towards Sir James and Mr. Hibbs," the detective continued, "what was Williams' attitude towards those two?"

She looked at her questioner and now stood directly in front of him, looking closely at him as though that question caused certain things to suddenly appear in her mind, things that had never occurred to her before that moment.

"My God!" she exclaimed, "you've made me think of something: I recall now that, when my father was alive, Williams seemed to ignore both Mr. Hibbs and Sir James. Oh, he was always extremely polite towards them, of course, but would refuse to render them any service that hadn't been specifically ordered by my father. Father and I would often be amused at this; we used to say to each other that Williams seemed to be quite closely attached to our family, such was his loyalty. And, since my father's death, Williams, despite living with us, has never been exactly gracious in serving Sir James or Mr. Hibbs. However, nobody has ever wished to dispense with his services."

She was astonished to now notice that the detective was quietly laughing, as though that answer of hers caused him some great moral or intellectual satisfaction.

"Perfect," he said, "all of that is extremely interesting to me, and I can see into your past life, perhaps better than even you yourself can see it. However, there is something else. Forgive me for telling you this, for it's extremely delicate. I have found...let's just say that it was by chance, in an open drawer, a strange I.O.U. Your father had borrowed money from..." He hesitated a moment. "...from Williams..."

Lucile had definitely known nothing of that, for she appeared dumbfounded.

Burke judged that he couldn't detain Lucile any longer in this icy-cold garden, and he led the young woman back into the house. They were about to go up the steps leading to the threshold when, by a sort of peculiarity of his character, he asked her one final question, and in a quite extraordinary manner.

He had reserved this parting shot till the end of his interview, and it was as if it were a somewhat theatrical effect, destined to act sharply on the young woman's brain.

He caught her shoulders, held her eyes fixed on his, and in a serious voice, a little severe, all affection having suddenly disappeared from his heart, he said: "Listen carefully. There are five people who can be regarded as suspects in the murder of Sir Roger: Williams, Sir James, Arthur Hibbs, you…and me. Which of those suspects seems, to you, the most likely?"

"But," she stammered, "I don't know what you expect me to say."

He urged her: "Answer me; I order you to do so."

So, staggering, unsteady on her feet, leaning against one side of the door towards which he guided her, she replied, but in such a low voice that Burke barely heard her: "Well…since I must tell you the truth, I thought it was…yes…I thought it was *you*."

Mr. Burke smiled; a strange smile. He let go of the young woman and, opening the door to allow her to enter, he said to her, with the utmost civility: "But…that wasn't at all poor reasoning on your part; I might have thought the same thing, had I been in your position."

And, instead of following Lucile, he closed the door behind her, remained a moment on the steps and lit a cigar.

Her room was situated on the first floor of the house, almost directly opposite Sir James', and, as she made her way there, she couldn't help thinking: "How can I have dared to reply in that manner? How could I have ever thought that he had killed my father? He is a good man…I'm sure of it…a very good man."

Suddenly, she started with fright.

She had just realized that her cousin Hibbs had been walking alongside her for several seconds without her noticing him.

Surprised, she turned towards him.

And the young man was wearing a strained, forced smile. "Yes," he murmured, "he's a good man, I don't disagree with you on that point, but he is perhaps a little 'less good' a man than you suppose him to be."

She then realized that she had been speaking aloud, and wondered if she hadn't broken the promise she'd made to Mr. Burke.

Arthur didn't give her any time to recover her composure. He said to her: "In any case, that 'good man' seeks to monopolize and manipulate you, and that seems to me to be, at the very least, strange. Be honest with me, Lucile, what was he saying to you just now in the garden? I saw you both through my window and your conversation seemed most interesting; he was holding you by the arm and speaking into your ear..."

The young woman made no reply, and so he repeated his question, one that was clearly of the utmost importance to him.

"What was he saying to you?"

She remained silent.

"So," he said, sarcastically, "despite everything I told you yesterday, you continue to trust this man? I'll have you know that I trust him even less today than I did yesterday! I'll say it again: why didn't he want to call in the police? And that would mean nothing, if I hadn't noticed that he now seeks to intimidate you; he wants to make you part of his little games and acquire an ally against me, against all of us...you're allowing yourself to be won over, and I feel you're distancing yourself from me because he has been blaming me for God knows what misdeeds...and you believe him!"

Hurt, she retorted: "Oh! Arthur, how can you say such things? You must know that he states for a fact that my father was murdered by somebody in this very house!"

She immediately wished she could take back those words that basically constituted the main secret Burke had confided in her, but it was too late. Moreover, Arthur appeared so upset that he had stopped questioning her. He repeated: "Murdered! You're saying...you believe your father to have been murdered by somebody in this household?"

Under no circumstances would Lucile have revealed anything more but, now, the young man was talking to himself. He was in thrall to a sort of turmoil and panic that Lucile couldn't account for, but one that made him look around to check that nobody was spying on them. He went on:

"I can see what you're thinking, Lucile; you're convinced that I too believed it was suicide, and you're wondering why I haven't gone along with your view of the matter over the past five years. You mustn't resent me for that; we're completely in the dark as to what really happened. You must know now that I too believe it was murder; but all the same, I never suspected that Burke would be impertinent enough to tell you all that himself...so he maintains that the murderer is, or was, somebody in our midst. That's very shrewd of him, but it's also madness on his part; madness that allows me to form an even better judgement of him."

VII

Where It Is Still a Question of Vampires...

AT EIGHT O'CLOCK in the evening; that is, when dinner had ended, Burke assembled his council of war one more time before nightfall.

That is, he gathered together, in the drawing room, all who resided in the house, and set out what he expected of them.

Betty, Williams and Harris kept themselves in the background, behind their masters, and remained standing.

Burke surveyed his associates – or his suspects, perhaps – and began by delivering a sort of mini-lecture to which everybody else listened in silence.

"I have made you a promise," he said, "to promptly solve this case, and I believe that there is now nothing to prevent me from finally delivering on that promise by tomorrow morning. Indeed, there have been fresh developments. The new tenants of Sir Roger's house came this evening to take occupation of the premises, probably on a permanent basis."

Hibbs shrugged his shoulders and, interrupting the detective, remarked coldly:

"They were even there yesterday, since you were able to speak to them."

Burke didn't appear to hear him, and continued: "I would appreciate no further interruptions, if you please. However, to answer Mr. Hibbs, I will admit that I went alone to the house next door last night and asked to be granted admittance therein, which was refused."

"Who did you meet there?" asked Arthur.

The detective shrugged his shoulders. "The principal tenant, to be precise. The man known as "the professor", whose silent chuckling made such a significant, spine-chilling impression on the solicitor...and on me. Having said this much, please be so kind as to not interrupt me any further; not another word, if you please."

The room once again fell silent.

"This evening, therefore, we're going to divide up the necessary tasks amongst us. I demand absolute obedience, and it is very important to me that nobody act according to their own personal whims. There is one single commander at the helm, which is myself; that's what I expect you to understand."

Mr. Hibbs permitted himself a snigger that the detective chose to ignore.

"Yes, absolute and passive obedience. You are all to remain confined to your rooms, all except Sir James, whom I now need. You shall be free to sleep if you so wish (and can); you shall even be able to read, or to accept visitors to your room, but I absolutely forbid you all to leave the house unless I so order you. I am now about to ask each of you, in person, to make a solemn promise to comply with those instructions."

He did as he had said, and Williams, Betty, Harris, Sir James and Lucile, each in turn, swore to observe the regulations as established by the detective.

Arthur proved more difficult in this respect; he began by stating that he saw no point in binding himself by an oath that, as far as he was concerned, he felt inclined to disregard. His ill-humour had a curious effect on the others and ultimately went against him.

Lucile besought him to act in accordance with the detective's orders, but the young man remained stubbornly determined in his absolute refusal to allow himself to be constrained to accept a form of authority that he hadn't asked for and wasn't willing to recognize.

The curious thing is that Mr. Burke didn't appear offended by this refusal and simply stated that, since Mr. Hibbs didn't wish to devote himself to the common good, there was no choice but to allow him to act as he saw fit.

"The one thing I *do* ask of you, however," he said, "Mr. Hibbs, is that you be here when I need you in the course of the night and that you not refuse to assist me."

The young man stood up and went to offer his hand to Mr. Burke, but the handshake he gave was certainly not a friendly one. It was almost as if, in actual fact, having taken the detective's hand, he didn't at all wish to let it go. He shook it with a sort of fury, and he spoke through his teeth as he replied, with simmering, barely-contained rage: "With all my heart I agree to your terms, my dear Sir. And, if you will permit it, I myself shall have some questions to ask of *you*, and I believe our interview shall be extremely interesting."

The detective bowed with a smile.

"I'm convinced that it will indeed be so, Mr. Hibbs. "You're a truly gifted conversationalist. The hours shall go by pleasantly in your company."

And that was all.

The servants were allowed to leave the room; Lucile and Arthur also withdrew so that only Sir James and Mr. Burke now remained in the drawing room.

The detective then proceeded to give particular instructions to him whom he had chosen to be his companion in that night's investigations; and what he had to ask of him was quite simple, even though, truth be told, the planned undertaking was not lacking either in unforeseen dangers or even in perils of a more predictable sort.

It was quite simply a matter of going to make an incursion into the house next door and, if they weren't able to get inside, they would observe, from the outside, what was going on indoors.

"I've anticipated the possibility that we might have to do combat," said Mr. Burke. "I'm giving you this revolver, Sir James, and I simply ask you to use it only in an extreme emergency, and only for the purposes of self-defense, should the need arise. Moreover, you can count on me to proceed with extreme caution."

He paused.

"I know" – he stressed that last word – "that Sir Roger Bradford is to be found inside the house next door."

He ignored the shivers that now went through Sir James' body, and continued:

"The only thing is, he isn't at all alone in there; as far as I'm concerned, we're going to find him in the company of four or five others."

Sir James raised his eyes to look at Mr. Burke.

"Real people?" he asked.

Mr. Burke lifted his hands; no doubt he didn't wish to compromise himself.

"I presume so," he said. "And I also presume that you have no more belief in ghosts today than you had yesterday?"

The other man shook his head.

"I no longer know what to believe," he murmured, "for isn't the world now upside down – is the ground we're walking on even solid?"

Mr. Burke didn't consider it appropriate to say any more or to state whether he thought the ground was still solid or not. He led his companion onwards; Sir James thus followed him at a certain distance behind, glancing fearfully around as he walked.

By this time, they had reached the mansion that had formerly been owned by Lucile's father, without having encountered anything that might have led them to believe that their purpose had been guessed at.

They stopped near a holly bush.

"Up there – look!"

It was Burke who had just spoken. He pointed to a window on the first floor and Sir James, nervously looking up, glimpsed through the glass of the window panes a diffuse glow, as if, inside that room, a covered lamp was radiating soft light all round it.

"There's somebody in there!"

Sir James had murmured those words and, as if what he'd seen prevented him from wishing to go any further, he remained frozen, rooted to the spot, not seeming to hear the detective's injunctions to move ahead with caution and without making any noise.

He nonetheless resolved to continue moving forward, but Burke was obliged to take him by the arm to help him ascend the steps leading up to the entrance of the mansion; even so, Sir James stumbled against the edges of the steps a few times.

It was not the investigator's intention to confine himself to a mere summary observation and, since there was somebody in the house, he was determined at all costs to find out who it was.

The window from which light was issuing was, as has been mentioned, on the first floor.

It would have been difficult to reach the first floor landing of the house without going by the staircase inside and Sir James pointed this out to his guide, whilst also informing him categorically that under no circumstances would he agree to accomplish that heroic exploit which consisted in breaking into the premises.

"You mean to tell me that you're afraid of your own tenants?" exclaimed Mr. Burke good-humouredly. "Remember, you're going to have to go to them to collect your rent…Or perhaps it's those animals that are making you uneasy?"

He pointed out the bats flying all around the dwelling, and facetiously observed that they were creatures which had been perfectly classified in natural history and which, in the opinion of all naturalists, had never caused the slightest harm to any living being.

"What's more," he added, "we won't have to go inside Sir Roger's house. Look to your right; there you will see a ladder that I made ready in the course of the afternoon; all we'll have to do is bring it a little nearer to the veranda so as to avoid any excessive risk of being spotted by the people inside."

As he spoke, he moved the ladder and continuously kept a close eye on his companion, for fear that he might suddenly try to make a bolt for it.

He made him pass in front of him and helped him to climb the ladder that he had, just now, noiselessly brought close to the veranda.

Sir James climbed over the balustrade with some difficulty and was thus the first to set foot on the stone platform. He was clearly getting weaker, and perhaps at that moment Burke was sorry for having forced him into such a proceeding in the dead of night.

"Here we are," he murmured.

Both of them had now taken up position on the veranda and kept prudently back from the illuminated window, so as not to be seen from inside should anyone happen to look in their direction.

Taking the utmost precautions, and allowing Sir James the time to recover from his exertions, the detective moved close to the window pane, got down on his knees to the stone surface and, for a long time, observed what was happening in the room.

In the past it had been Sir Roger's bedroom, and in those days it had been a fine room. Some of the furniture was still there, except the bed and the large armchairs that had been removed in order to be reassembled in Sir James' house.

But around the great table that still occupied the centre of the room, a weird company was gathered.

Burke seemed to take great pleasure in studying all those who were there, and in watching their every movement. He was extremely interested in what he saw, but didn't betray any feelings of fear or bewilderment.

Turning towards Sir James, he spoke to him in a calm, gentle voice:

"Well! All that is perfectly normal. I'm certain you won't be at all frightened if you take a look yourself. Take my place at the window, will you?"

Sir James, led forward by the detective's hand, knelt in his turn and went to place his forehead against the window pane. The reassuring manner in which Burke had spoken had obviously not prepared Sir James for the extraordinary sight he was about to witness, and when he saw the scene within the room with his own eyes, he remained rooted to the spot, paralyzed with fear, gasping and unable to move.

Exactly opposite him, he could see his cousin, Sir Roger!

This time, there could be no mistaking the evidence of his own eyes. The dead man's face was completely illuminated by the light from a lamp that hung from the ceiling and, even though he wasn't moving, despite the fact that his face was perfectly still, he was clearly…alive.

His eyes, riveted to this macabre tableau, followed part of the scene that was unfolding around the table. No, this wasn't at all a dead man, but a truly living individual.

Sir James' teeth began to clatter.

Right beside Sir Roger, there stood that character who had caused such agitation in the solicitor, the professor who chuckled constantly. His ghastly white complexion was not at all that of living human beings. Had he risen from his grave to attend this weirdest of gatherings?

But the thing that struck Sir James perhaps even more forcibly was the bizarre face of the woman who stood behind the professor. That woman had nothing at all lifelike about her, in either her person or her face. It was as though she were a spectre that had issued forth from its tomb, a fleshless, pitiful, ghastly apparition.

Sir James couldn't take his eyes off those three creatures, and he was probably unable to marvel at anything else, for the detective, placing his finger right on the window to point at something, now drew his attention to a more distant point of the bedroom, saying:

"And down there? There's something down there that I can't make out very clearly. Might you be able to tell me what it is?"

No, Sir James couldn't explain what it was, because, at that very moment, he collapsed backwards and the detective had to catch him in his arms.

The thing Sir James had seen wasn't, perhaps, anything very remarkable, and perhaps it might have been nothing at all to him if his mind hadn't already been full of the recent discussions on the subject of vampires.

For the terrible thing he had noticed was like a floating ectoplasm endowed with beating wings, and which was moving about at the rear of the bedroom between the ceiling and the floor.

Sir James fell with a heavy thud and his companion had to slap him about the cheeks to revive him.

And when Sir James opened his eyes, still full of the nightmare he had just experienced, he stammered:

"Burke, let's get out of here; there's nothing we can do against such creatures."

"That's just about what I was thinking too," replied Burke, without giving any additional explanation.

And he led the cousin of the dead man who had returned to life, back to his own house and told Sir James that he was giving him the rest of the night to recover from his ordeal.

The detective noticed that, although Mr. Hibbs had refused to swear an oath, he hadn't left his room; and he summoned him, as well as Lucile, to the drawing room.

Sir James was present but, collapsed on a couch, didn't seem able to shed any light whatsoever on what he had seen, nor to recount what he had just done.

Burke thus gave a brief account and declared that in his opinion, the house next door was filled with people who might have struck terror into anybody less sceptical than he himself was.

Arthur had listened to this description of events without offering any opinion. However, when the detective had finished, he said, with a certain air of casual indifference: "Don't you think, my dear Detective, that if somebody was trying at all costs to prevent us from gaining entry to the house next door, they would have come up with some better way[1] of attaining their ends? After the account you've just given us, who in their right mind would dare to go and see what was happening inside Sir Roger's house?"

Then, having paused for a moment, he went on in a slightly lower voice:

---

1. The sense of the passage, in context, would indicate that Hibbs is asking whether there would have been a *simpler* or *less complicated* way for that "somebody" – even one endeavoring "at all costs"--to prevent access to the house next door, for Hibbs goes on immediately to remark how extraordinarily effective the present "way" has proven to be – i.e., there is, therefore, no need for it to be "better" or more effective than it has already proven to be. Similarly, however, in Part Two, Section II, Burke's associate Bryce, referring to the complexity of the whole plan, asks him specifically, "wasn't there a simpler way…?"; and there Burke answers, "Old friend, don't worry yourself about what might have been simpler or more complicated; as you can imagine, I had my reasons for going about things in this way, even though you don't understand them as yet." Thus the sense of Hibbs' question here is quite the same as Bryce's later; but here the French term used by Hibbs is indeed *meilleur* (rather than Bryce's *plus simple*), which is accurately translated as "better" rather than "simpler". Any confusion of expression here, then, then, is attributable to the novelist, not to the translator. –TM.

"And who on earth would, more specifically, go next door to see whether there's still any evidence of the murder committed five years ago?"

Burke gave a strange look at the young man and, without taking his eyes from him, said to him in a low voice:

"Not even you, I presume?"

Arthur took a step backwards.

"No," he said, shivering, "no, you're right! Not even I would dare to do such a thing."

It had been agreed that, during this final part of the investigation, everybody would have the right to speak, and the distances that usually separated masters and servants would be temporarily erased. For were not all of the inhabitants of the house linked to each other by a common concern for self-defense against the mysterious terror that hovered, threatening all of them?

Betty, benefitting from this permission to speak, ventured to give her opinion. She believed more strongly than ever in vampires and relied on Mr. Hibbs' testimony, Mr. Hibbs being a cultured and most learned gentleman who had studied all branches of science.

"Sir," she said to Burke, "I don't know what you think about all this, nor what you believe but, as far as I'm concerned, my mind is made up; I read in the book that Mr. Hibbs was reading the other day that people used to protect themselves against vampires by placing a sharp, pointed sword and a wreath of tuberoses in the lock of the door to one's sleeping quarters. Well! Tonight, whether you like it or not, I'm going to do as the book says, at least for my own bedroom, and as I'm also responsible for Lady Lucile, I want you to allow me to provide the same protection at her own bedroom door."

Burke looked at her without smiling.

"So do you have enough swords and a sufficient quantity of tuberoses?" he asked.

She replied:

"Begging your pardon, Sir, Harris went to the flower stall at the market today and he's brought me back as many tuberoses as we need to protect the whole house!"

And Harris, who was standing in a corner of the room, didn't at all contradict her.

"I've spent my whole afternoon making up wreaths," he said. "There's enough to fill an entire graveyard and the smell is so strong in the kitchen that there's no way we could eat there this evening, everything tasted so much of tuberoses."

"As for swords," Betty went on, "I've found only one, but swords can easily be replaced by chopping knives; I imagine they'll do the job just as well, since they're sharp."

Burke looked at the cook with the same seriousness as before.

"Well," he said, "since you believe that this can protect Miss Lucile, I'll help you, my dear woman; and, if it's all the same to you, I myself will take care of securing your mistress's bedroom. Go and fetch your wreaths and your knives, and also your book."

Betty was most satisfied.

In truth, she hadn't thought she would meet with such resounding success, and the night ahead now seemed less bleak, dismal and threatening.

Just as Burke had requested, they began by defending Lucile's room against evil supernatural forces. First of all, the window was barred by a sword, upon which the detective hung the wreath.

Then, as if all those who now surrounded him were hindering him in his efforts, he asked them to go away.

Arthur Hibbs didn't take too kindly to this order, and made his protests clear. As the detective was urging him once more to leave the room, he replied sarcastically:

"For someone who doesn't believe in vampires, you seem to be taking a significant interest in them, it seems to me?"

And Burke retorted in the same tone: "Probably for the same reasons as you, Mr. Hibbs. But, never fear, I shall go and chat to you about all that in half an hour. Will you be so kind as to go and wait for me in your room?"

"I was going to ask you if we could talk later," replied the young man, "and I give you my oath that I shan't fall asleep before you come."

He then went out quickly, and the detective, having half-closed the door, listened and watched through the opening to ensure that nobody had remained in the corridor to furtively observe him.

The hall was deserted.

Mr. Burke thus closed the door fully and went over to Lucile who was waiting, standing beside her bed.

"Be brave, my dear young woman, and answer me frankly; do you still trust me?"

She allowed the detective to take her hand.

"Still, and always, Mr. Burke."

He made her sit down on a sofa and he then sat beside her.

"You will have to follow my instructions to the letter," he began. "First of all, if I'm not mistaken, I believe that you still have that little white and pink dress you were wearing the evening your father was killed?"

She still had it, indeed, but she was astonished that he knew this.

"Who told you?"

Without waiting for a reply, the young woman thought for a moment.

"But," she murmured, "how will I be able to leave my room, since the door and the window have both been sealed? For I presume that the things you've placed at my window have no other use than to make it impossible to get in or out?"

Burke nodded in confirmation.

"You're absolutely right. For that reason you are not going to remain in your room. Before I close the door, you will have gone out and you will have gone to the dining room where I have set you up comfortably. You know that, in that room, there is a covered balcony where, in times gone by, musicians used to perform on special days of great celebration. It is masked by a curtain and will provide a shelter that, if not comfortable, is at least perfectly concealed. I have myself put a sofa there, on which you can rest. Now, listen carefully."

Lucile waited attentively, unmoving.

"From three o'clock in the morning onwards, as I've told you, try to remain awake because Betty will come and fetch you, to bring you into the house next door. Do you promise to obey me?"

Once more, Lucile shook the detective's hand.

"I promise," she said. "I'm now sure that you will discover who killed my father."

Part Two

While Smoking a Cigar

ARTHUR HIBBS wasn't sleeping; he was waiting for Mr. Burke as he had promised.

He chose a book at random and allowed it to fall open casually.

Arthur Hibbs was reading a page of a novel for the second time without understanding its meaning, because his distracted mind was elsewhere, when there came a soft tap on the door.

It was Burke. He said:

"May I ask you, Mr. Hibbs, if I can smoke one of your excellent cigars with you, so we can begin the interview I requested of you and proceed in comfort?"

The young man agreed but without much good grace. And Burke sat down on an armchair opposite him.

"You don't trust me, Mr. Hibbs – am I right?"

The young man replied with the same tone:

"And your distrust of me is even greater, Mr. Burke – am I right?"

And both men, without really knowing why, began to laugh, after which they fell silent, an awkward, heavy silence that would perhaps have been excessively prolonged, had the detective not continued:

"Could you explain the reasons why you think I might have killed Sir Roger?"

Arthur Hibbs put all his cards on the table. "Because," he replied, "I know that all of the bearer securities that Sir Roger had left to his daughter disappeared from his house on the day of the murder; because I think that a man who was gotten rid of by Scotland Yard, as you were, for reasons that nobody wants to reveal, may very well be a dishonest man, and because nothing about your means of investigation is clear."

Burke nodded. "And must I tell you, Mr. Hibbs, that it's also that very reason, amongst lots of others, which made me suspect you; you who take such evident pleasure in making everything that is clear seem confusing and murky. Yes, I did suspect you."

The young man gave a start.

"What!" he exclaimed, "You mean you no longer suspect me?"

"Not for the moment," the detective replied, "but I may very well suspect you once again, in a quarter of an hour."

"Perhaps you still wish to conduct a search of my room?"

"No, not in the slightest. The only reason I've come to your room this evening is to have a chat with you. You've just now made reference to my resignation from Scotland Yard, and you've cast doubt on my integrity; I don't need to justify myself to you, of course; however, I imagine you'd like to know why I left the official police force."

"I would be greatly obliged to you if you would tell me," the young man replied, "but I obviously don't have the power to force you to do so."

Burke paused; his grey, deep-set eyes seemed to throw out a sharp flame. And he said:

"Quite simply because I believe in hypnotism..."

"Oh!" exclaimed Arthur. "You believe in it?

"One has no choice but to believe in it," the detective continued, "when one has, like me, more evidence than one knows what to do with. It is thanks to the power of hypnosis that I have obtained my greatest successes in criminal investigation, but I must admit that this method isn't part of the usual procedures of our British police force. The individual liberty of human beings is sacrosanct, as you know, and every criminal has the right not to say anything, if he doesn't think it's useful to his defense. To extract from him, by a scientific method, the decisive admission of guilt that his conscience forbids him to make is not considered compelling evidence. But, my dear Sir, I swear to you that I've never used this method, save in exceptional cases and always in a perfectly controlled manner. Before continuing our conversation on the matter that is of concern to you, allow me to ask you whether, in all sincerity, you would be willing to let me place you in a hypnotic trance this evening?"

This was clearly the most serious question that Mr. Burke had asked since he had first entered Sir James' house.

Arthur Hibbs reflected for a few moments and as Burke watched him intently, he rose from his armchair and, his hand placed flat on his table, as though on that very spot there was a Bible on which he was swearing an oath, he replied, frankly and distinctly:

"Sir, I agree with the English police and I'm fervently opposed to any methods that deprive a human being – even a criminal – of their free will. Nevertheless, I would be completely willing to allow you to hypnotize me if I were absolutely convinced that you were an honest man. Unfortunately, I don't have that conviction."

"Not bad," said the detective. "To put it plainly, you refuse."

"Yes, I refuse, because it's you who have asked me to submit to that experiment! I'm not stating for a fact that you *are* Sir Roger's killer, but I don't trust you, that's all."

Burke seemed to take these words in very good spirit.

"You may have a reason," he said, "but I am forced to note that you are refusing to give me the only proof I might have of your innocence. Your argument is very clever on the surface, but, for me, it's the same as if you'd said 'No' to me without giving me any good reason."

He lowered his voice slightly and continued speaking, very softly, very calmly, and his voice seemed to have undergone a complete transformation because it was cloaked in delicate undertones and seemed to sing musically in Arthur's ears:

"And yet, what a wonderful subject of hypnosis you might have been! You have the gift of dreams, Mr. Hibbs; you are an imaginative person, an artist; you sometimes live in a domain that remains hidden from the eyes of other human beings, you're interested in vampires, if only from a strictly poetic point of view…"

In a daze, the young man listened and seemed to be paying more attention to the detective's voice than to his actual words.

There was, in that voice, something which was having a striking effect upon him. Its delicate inflections modulated from deep to soft, and it was akin to a languorous, lulling, but slightly childish sound.

How could Burke, ordinarily so incisive and curt, now be speaking so entrancingly?

And he continued:

"People have strange ideas about hypnosis, my dear Sir; they think it's brutal whereas in fact it's all about patience and gentleness. Look into my eyes: are they malicious? No they aren't, are they? All you see there is trust and security; your own are as lucid as calm waters reflecting the sky overhead."

He had come nearer to the young man. With his fingers, he gently brushed his face and eyebrows.

Arthur Hibbs felt this touch without being in the least discommoded, he showed no reaction; he listened and, despite himself, gazed at the detective.

If he had had to say where he was at that moment, he would have been unable to. The objects in his bedroom that he knew so well because he had himself arranged them, were disappearing in a sort of fog; the walls seemed to be moving further away and now everything began to slowly whirl round while he wondered if he was being carried off on some magical and infinitely enjoyable merry-go-round.

And now, suddenly, he could no longer hear anything. He could see the detective's lips moving but all he could distinguish on his face was his look, which shone with such intensity that it seemed as though it were the only thing that truly existed in front of him.

He fell gently onto the armchair from which he had risen a moment before. But he wasn't even aware that he was sitting down; he had lost all consciousness. He had been transported into an extraordinary world of divine light and silvery sounds.

He was sleeping. He was now in the power of Mr. Burke.

* * *

"Well," murmured Burke, mopping his brow, "that wasn't easy but I got there in the end. These fellows thinks they're shielded against everything, but it's just pure vanity on their part."

He was perfectly satisfied with his work. Without the young man suspecting a thing, the detective had put him into a state of third-degree slumber, the state in which the subject gives himself over, body and soul, to the person who has mesmerized him; a state of perfect susceptibility.

What was Burke going to do?

He began by prolonging the slumber through applying downward touches to the face and chest. Then, grasping the young man with both hands, he stretched him out onto the sofa so that he would be completely comfortable and wouldn't suffer at all from being in a tiring posture; then, gravely, as he spoke, not as though to a sleeping person but to a man who was completely aware and self-willed, he explained:

"Listen to me, Mr. Hibbs, you must hear me, I order you to hear me...can you hear me?"

The young man's lips opened slightly and Burke felt rather than distinctly heard the "Yes" that emanated therefrom.

He went on:

"You must know that I have greater respect for due process than you yourself imagine; I could, at this very moment, ask you whether or not you killed Sir Roger, but I won't do it. It is a matter for your own free will, as you were saying earlier, to decide and to reply. But nothing prevents me from having you relive the night of the crime. Recall that night, Hibbs, recall it! You have now gone back five years into the past. You are now in the exact spot where you were on the day Sir Roger was murdered. You understand me clearly, *you are* the person *you were* five years ago; think of that and don't move!"

A change had come about on the young man's face; his features had been tense, but as the detective spoke, they relaxed and reassumed their natural expression.

The detective noticed this change and stopped.

"Now," he said to himself, "we are going to move on to another sort of procedure. This dear young fellow is going to enjoy the sleep of the just until I decide to wake him; that'll soften up his character!"

He looked for something in the room, and, finally, took a blanket from the bed. He spread it over the young man's sleeping frame, so that he would be completely hidden from view, and only allowed him enough room around his face to breathe freely. After which, removing his own jacket and shoes, he quite simply lay down on Mr. Arthur Hibbs' bed.

Williams Hears a Gunshot

BURKE WAS STILL IN THE BED but he wasn't sleeping.

Wrapped in the blankets, he was simply waiting for something.

But he probably hadn't expected what actually then took place. The lights were completely extinguished, the detective was musing on the fact that it's sometimes hard to stay awake, even when you're a good hypnotist and could easily influence yourself in the sense desired by the situation - by preventing yourself from falling asleep, and thus staying awake a whole night, for example.

He had just heard the clock strike two a.m.; and, if everything went according to plan, he still had another hour to remain there before going downstairs. But then, during that hour, the unexpected event that has just been mentioned, indeed occurred.

Burke had just turned his head on the pillow, when it seemed to him that the bedroom door was being gently opened.

He watched carefully, and realized that he wasn't the victim of an optical illusion.

Between the door and the wall, the dimmed light coming from the hall slid across in front of him and a light-coloured shadow was growing larger on the carpet.

Taking care not to make the slightest sound, Burke moved across the bed to position himself on its edge, from where he had a better view.

The open door was not opposite him and he therefore was unable to distinguish the person pushing it.

But, as soon as the door was open wide enough, Burke saw a hand advancing and that hand was holding an object that the detective recognized. He squashed himself against the mattress, making himself as small as he possibly could. And just at that very moment, a shot rang out and a bullet, grazing the bedside table that was placed in front of the bed, struck the pillow at a hair's breadth from the detective's head, and immediately the door slammed, hastily shut.

Burke was already on his feet. He ran to the door, opened it and looked into the hall.

There was nobody to be seen.

Then, taking his revolver, he moved forward cautiously, inspecting every nook and cranny, and reached the landing without noticing anything suspicious.

He listened.

From the ground floor he could hear the sound of footsteps; he went downstairs and found himself, so to speak, face to face with Williams, who was quickly putting on his coat.

The detective seized the butler by the hand.

"Where are you going?"

Williams started in fright.

"Sir," he said, "I heard a gunshot barely five minutes ago!"

"Where were you when you heard this gunshot?"

"In my room, on the third floor."

"Just as I thought. So, you heard, from your room, a gunshot that has just been fired from the first floor. Do you know what that means, Williams?"

The butler, taken aback, shook his head.

"No, Sir."

"It means that the day Sir Roger was murdered, you lied to me. If you recall, you claimed to have gone downstairs to check on your master, driven by some supernatural force; yet the layout of this house is the same as that of the house next door. In that house too, your room was on the third floor and your master was killed on the first floor. Therefore, you came downstairs because you heard the gunshot and, I repeat, you lied to me."

Williams had retreated into the shadows of the stairwell; the detective could see his trembling figure but didn't spare him.

And Williams spoke, like someone completely stricken by panic and fear.

"Sir," he said, "I know what you must think, but I'm not guilty, I swear to you that I didn't do anything wrong that day; and *this* evening, it was because I heard a gunshot that I came downstairs, I don't know who fired it..."

He continued to repeat the same denials and Burke, leading him back into the light, studied him from head to toe, pausing to examine his hands a little more carefully than his face.

The butler submitted to this observation without protest, but his feeling of uneasiness was increasing.

And Burke, no longer studying him, suddenly said:

"In any case, if it's any relief to you, I can assure you that I'm not at all accusing you of firing the fatal shot that night because your hand…"

He didn't finish his thought. A strange smile hovered on his lips.

He went on.

"I'm going to ask you to remain in your room, Williams. If you do as I say, nothing unpleasant will happen to you, but in an hour or two, I'm going to need your help. If someone comes looking for you on my orders, follow that person."

And Burke calmly went back up to the first floor.

Sir James stood in the corridor; the master of the house appeared frightened, anxiety-stricken. Seeing the detective, he ran to him and cried:

"Who fired that shot? Where did that gunshot come from?"

Burke shrugged his shoulders.

"I have no idea," he said, "but my impression now is that the sound came from your nephew's room. I thought at first it was from the ground floor and I went downstairs with Williams…yes, he was awake – but there's nothing down there that need concern us. Quick, let's go and see what has become of Mr. Hibbs."

They knocked on Arthur's door, but the detective went in there on his own, and came out immediately, saying:

"He isn't in his bed."

Sir James' eyes blinked rapidly.

"My God!" he exclaimed, "what's happened? Why isn't Arthur there?"

"That's what I want to know," replied Mr. Burke, "I've been waiting for him for three hours and there hasn't been sight nor sound of him. I'm as worried as you are."

Then, unhurriedly, and proceeding in a manner that exhibited his perfectly methodical mind, he took a small notebook from his pocket; and, looking over some handwritten notes written in pencil that indicated all he had planned to do, he read:

1. Make all the residents of this house go to the house next door. In the first place, Lucile.

He closed his notebook and went upstairs to the servants' quarters.

He was looking for a particular bedroom and stopped outside a door on which a number had been inscribed.

He knocked gently.

The door was immediately opened, and Betty appeared.

She was dressed and ready to leave.

In fact, the Betty who now presented herself was completely different to the woman they were accustomed to seeing in the house. An intelligent light shone in her eyes and she didn't seem in the least alarmed by ghosts or vampires.

As she listened to Mr. Burke, she calmly adjusted her hat, buttoned her coat and solidly tied her shoelaces.

"So, Betty," went on Mr. Burke, "all that you have to do now is to follow my orders exactly. You know what has to be done here and next door, don't you?"

The cook replied clearly, and without her usual flustered verbosity:

"I remember everything you've said, Sir; you can count on me."

"Good. So, go and fetch Lady Lucile in the covered balcony of the dining room. You will take her to Sir Roger's house, but above all, don't frighten her, and you will introduce her to the people there. Most importantly, say what you have to, but not a word more."

Betty made a sign to show she'd understood.

"This is good work, Betty. You are an assistant worthy of promotion, and my report to Inspector Bryce will be completely favourable to you, praising your abilities; rest assured of that."

She replied, without any sign of emotion on her face.

"Thank you, Mr. Burke; a reference from you will, moreover, be very useful to me, because I've applied to become part of the counter-espionage brigade."

"But," the detective went on, "we'll talk a little later about our private affairs. For now, we have something else to concern ourselves with. Go and do your duty, Betty, and when you're in the house next door, hide yourself so that nobody from this house, meaning Sir James and Mr. Hibbs, can see you."

He went back up to the first floor and went into the room where he had left Arthur asleep on the sofa.

Bending over the sleeping body, Burke applied several touches from the heart upwards to the forehead.

At the same time, he murmured to him, in a voice that was becoming more and more distinct, louder and louder:

"Wake up, Mr. Hibbs, wake up! You've been sleeping...and remember...you are the man you were five years ago, the day Sir Roger was killed; it is nine o'clock in the evening."

Arthur began by moving his limbs slightly.

The detective touched the young man's eyelids, pressing quite strongly on the eyeball.

Then, when he felt Hibbs was about to come to, he put him in a natural seated position on the sofa while he himself, quickly helping himself to a cigar, lit it, and stood opposite the young man as if he were continuing a conversation that had begun earlier and that nothing had interrupted.

"To sum up," he was saying, "people think there's something brutal about hypnosis, but it's a completely patient, gentle process. Look into my eyes – do they seem malicious to you? No, they aren't, are they? And your own eyes are as clear as calm waters..."

These were, as the reader will remember, the last words that had been uttered before Mr. Hibbs' slumber and the latter, awakening, would think that no interval of time had separated the moment when he had been stretched out on the sofa, and the moment when he sat up again.

Seated on the sofa, he was looking at the detective as though at a man who has returned from some faraway place; so Burke seemed, certainly, yet the detective didn't seem at all surprised to find himself here.

And while Mr. Burke watched him carefully, the young man struggled to understand why he was experiencing a certain amount of difficulty in following the train of thought of the detective.

But Burke didn't appear to notice anything.

"At the end of the day," he continued, "you would make an excellent subject for hypnosis, but it shan't be me who will ever try to put you in a trance."

And he then leaned over slightly towards the young man and said to him, as though he had seen something surprising on his face:

"Forgive me!" he exclaimed, "I thought for a moment...well, it seemed as if you'd dozed off."

Arthur wiped his forehead with his hand.

"Indeed," he stammered. "Indeed, it's curious! I don't know what came over me just now...How long have you been standing there?"

Burke cast an astonished look in his direction.

"But...I've been here barely ten minutes. Don't you remember?"

"It's the strangest thing!" Arthur went on, "but there seems to be a blank in my memory."

"Look," the detective continued, "I can see you're tired so I won't bother you any further by remaining here."

He was just about to leave when the young man suddenly caught him by the arm. There was a change in his tone of voice and his vacant eyes seemed filled with anxiety.

"Burke!" he said, with a slightly hoarse voice, "answer me! What day is it today? What day? Quickly!"

"Don't worry about that," the detective replied. "It's of no importance whatsoever. Live as you are meant to live, and act without weighing up the consequences of your actions."

And, as he said this, he remained standing in the half-open door, watching the young man to see what he was going to do.

Once again, Arthur Hibbs wiped his forehead with his hand and looked round him as if he was searching for something, then, with a slow, mechanical step, he went towards the cabinet in which he had arranged his books and took one of them out, having first caressed the binding of each one of them. He was looking for a specific volume, undoubtedly the one that he had been reading on that evening which the detective had just made him begin to relive under hypnosis.

Burke half-closed the door, leaving it sufficiently ajar to enable him to continue keeping watch over Hibbs through the narrow opening.

He suddenly heard a dull thud and realized that the young man had just thrown his book onto the floor.

After which he had hurried out the door, and, having exited briskly, he was now pacing up the long corridor.

"Let's leave him be," said Burke, "and move on to a more urgent task."

He then went to knock softly on Sir James' door.

The master of the house opened it.

"Sir James," said Burke, "events are unfolding exactly as I had planned them, and the facts are following the progression I had assigned to them. Look at me, I want to check whether I can count on you; try to make your expression as calm as mine."

Sir James, baffled, obeyed the order and stared at Burke. He couldn't really understand what the detective was getting at.

Then, over the next few minutes, the detective spoke to him in a way that Sir James found astonishing, but Burke's speech was identical to the words he had already uttered earlier that evening in Mr. Hibbs' room.

His gentle and musical tones were like a soothing lullaby to which Sir James was undoubtedly very receptive, for his head was nodding and he didn't seem in the least puzzled by his guest's strange monologue. If he had understood, from the start, what Burke's purpose was, he might have reacted differently, but it was now too late.

And, little by little, he behaved exactly as Arthur had done. Subjected to hypnotic influences, he remained deprived of conscious thought, incapable of registering any protest, but he didn't at all fall asleep because Burke halted the experiment before sleep could take over. It was sufficient for his purposes that the master of the house be maintained in a state of wakefulness and that he be hypnotically receptive to the suggestions of the mesmerizing detective.

He then spoke in a clear and persuasive tone, with each of his words distinctly articulated:

"Sir James, you are in exactly the same spot that you were in five years ago, on the day that Sir Roger was murdered."

Twice more he repeated his suggestion and waited.

Sir James appeared to hesitate for a moment and began looking around his bedroom, after which, with deliberate steps, he left the room, took several steps in the corridor, all the while looking round as though he was fearful of being caught, and made his way towards a small room situated at the end of the hall, in which the household cleaning utensils were kept – Burke knew this. He took a key from this room – the key that opened the door in the boundary wall separating the two rear gardens.

"Good," said Burke, "all is going well."

And, allowing the various individuals to act as they intended, he hurried to the stairs and, running in order to reach the neighbouring dwelling before all the others who were logically due to go there too, he arrived in Sir Roger's residence.

His arrival had been expected.

In the damp and dilapidated front room, the professor with the silent chuckle seemed to be expecting his arrival, for he said:

"Ah! There you are, Mr. Burke; I was beginning to get worried at your tardiness."

Burke quickly removed his jacket and hung it on the coat rack.

Then, holding out his hands towards the tenant: "Quickly, my friend, pass me your Inverness cape and your false teeth."

"So, everything is going according to plan, Mr. Burke?"

"Yes, Bryce, yes, my old friend, and I believe this is going to be the crowning success of my entire career. We've got the nephew, the butler and the master of the house exactly where we want them. That whole vampire presentation that went on for three days, has shaken them so much that I think that we would have driven them all mad if we'd kept it up for a further twenty-four hours."

"Wasn't there any simpler way...?" began Bryce.

The detective interrupted him. "Old friend, don't worry yourself about what might have been simpler or more complicated; as you can imagine, I had my reasons for going about things in this way, even though you don't understand them as yet. Tell me now, where is the young lady whom our loyal Betty brought here?"

"She's with Luna," replied Bryce, "She doesn't seem to be too frightened; on the contrary, she's very impatient for you to reveal the truth to her."

"It won't be long now," replied the detective. "Bring me to her, will you?"

Photo : Metro Goldwyn Mayer.

Lucile, la propre fille unique de la victime.

Londres après Minuit. — 2.

Lucile, the victim's only daughter.

Photo : Metro Goldwyn Mayer.

Lucile vivait maintenant dans la maison de Sir James.

Londres après Minuit. — 5.

Lucile was now living in Sir James' house.

Photo : Metro Goldwyn Mayer.

Betty se précipita, suivie à quelques pas d'Harris.

Londres après Minuit. — 4.

Betty rushed in, followed at a few paces by Harris.

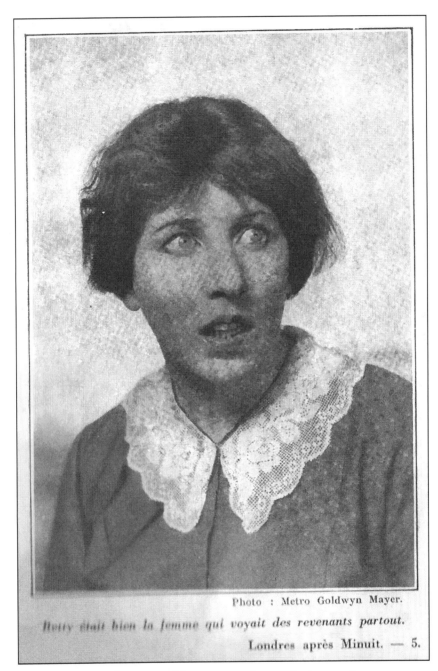

Photo : Metro Goldwyn Mayer.

Betty était bien la femme qui voyait des revenants partout.

Londres après Minuit. — 5.

Betty really was one of those women who saw ghosts everywhere.

Photo : Metro Goldwyn Mayer.

On revenait, Harris et moi, dans la voiture.

Londres après Minuit. — 6.

We were coming back, Harris and I, in the coach.

Photo : Metro Goldwyn Mayer.

On a vu deux ombres qui sortaient de la maison.

Londres après Minuit. — 7.

We saw two shadows coming out of the house.

Photo : Metro Goldwyn Mayer.

On aurait dit une morte sortie de sa tombe depuis peu.

Londres après Minuit. — 8.

One would almost have thought it was a dead woman who had just emerged from her tomb a short time previously.

Photo : Metro Goldwyn Mayer.

Au cours de la soirée on lui apporta une carte.

Londres après Minuit. — 9.

In the course of the evening, a card was brought to him.

Photo : Metro Goldwyn Mayer.

Maintenant, je vous demande de ne rien me cacher.

Londres après Minuit. — 10.

I now ask you not to hide anything from me.

Photo : Metro Goldwyn Mayer.

Ne craignez rien, mon enfant, je suis là.

Londres après Minuit. — 11.

Fear nothing, my child; I'm here.

Photo : Metro Goldwyn Mayer.

Ils partirent tous les trois.

Londres après Minuit. — 12.

The three of them set off.

Photo : Metro Goldwyn Mayer.

J'ai vu un hommes qui avait des ailes...

Londres après Minuit. — 13.

I saw a man with wings…

Photo : Metro Goldwyn Mayer.

Monsieur Burke, j'ai une grande confiance en vous.

Londres après Minuit. —— 14.

Mr. Burke, I have great trust in you.

J'étais tout pour mon père.

Londres après Minuit. — 15.

I was everything to my father.

Photo : Metro Goldwyn Mayer.

Les locataires de la maison de Sir Roger ont pris possession des locaux.

Londres après Minuit. — 16.

The tenants of Sir Roger's house have taken occupation.

Photo : Metro Goldwyn Mayer.

Juste en face de lui, il voyait son cousin, Sir Roger.

Londres après Minuit. — 17.

Right in front of him, he could see his cousin, Sir Roger.

Photo : Metro Goldwyn Mayer.

Une singulière figure de femme.

Londres après Minuit. — 18.

A most unusual feminine figure.

Photo : Metro Goldwyn Mayer.

La porte fut barrée d'une épée avec une couronne de tubéreuses.

Londres après Minuit. — 19.

The door was sealed with a sword and a wreath of tuberoses.

Photo : Metro Goldwyn Mayer.

De ses doigts il faisait des passes magnétiques.

Londres après Minuit. — 20.

With his fingers, he was applying magnetic touches.

Photo : Metro Goldwyn Mayer.

Burke vit une main s'avancer.

Londres après Minuit. — 21.

Burke saw a hand moving forward.

Photo : Metro Goldwyn Mayer.

Lorsqu'il le sentit prêt à reprendre connaissance...

Londres après Minuit. — 22.

When he felt him to be ready to regain consciousness…

Photo : Metro Goldwyn Mayer.

N'ayez aucune crainte, Miss Lucile, je suis là.

Londres après Minuit. — 23.

Fear nothing, Miss Lucile; I'm here.

Photo : Metro Goldwyn Mayer.

Voilà le neveu, le valet et le maître.

Londres après Minuit. — 24.

There are the nephew, the butler and the master.

Oui, c'est moi, Lucile, regardez-moi bien.

Londres après Minuit. — 25.

Yes, it's me, Lucile; take a good look at me.

Photo : Metro Goldwyn Mayer.

Luna était revêtue d'une longue tunique blanche.

Londres après Minuit. — 26.

Luna was dressed in a long white tunic.

Photo : Metro Goldwyn Mayer.

— *La cérémonie va commencer, dit Burke.*

Londres après Minuit. — 27.

"Let the ceremony begin," said Burke.

Photo : Metro Goldwyn Mayer.

*La jeune fille passive et abandonnée
accepta toutes les suggestions.*

Londres après Minuit. — 28.

The young woman, passive and submissive, accepted all his suggestions.

Photo : Metro Goldwyn Mayer.

Arthur et Lucile se tenaient les mains.

Londres après Minuit. — 29.

Arthur and Lucile were holding hands.

Photo : Metro Goldwyn Mayer.

Il était évident que Lucile ne pouvait en entendre davantage.

Londres après Minuit. — 30.

It was obvious that Lucile would be unable to listen to any more of this.

Photo : Metro Goldwyn Mayer.

— Je lui ai trouvé un déguisement propre à frapper les esprits.

Londres après Minuit. — 31.

"I found him a disguise quite apt to strike terror into the minds of all."

Photo : Metro Goldwyn Mayer.

— Lucile, voulez-vous me permettre de vous faire oublier ce cauchemar?

Londres après Minuit. — 32.

"Lucile, will you please allow me to make you forget this nightmare?"

III

In Which the Story Offers a Flashback To Five Years Previously

LUCILE, JUST AS SHE HAD promised Mr. Burke, followed Betty without hesitation and without displaying the slightest fear.

Both women left the house and were admitted into the neighbouring mansion.

And the young woman who was among the new tenants introduced herself:

"I'm the one they call Luna," she said. "You can trust me – please sit down!"

Luna wore a long white tunic; her complexion was extremely pale, but all that was merely the result of cleverly applied make-up, in the same way that her bright eyes had acquired their brilliance only because of the dark eye-shadow she was wearing.

Lucile sat down.

"Remember," said Luna, "that you're acting in your father's memory and in order to unmask his killer."

The young woman observed with curiosity the strange appearance of the house in which she had once lived. Those strange black veils, cut into bizarre shapes, hanging from the ceiling – weren't they shaped like bats' wings?

At one particular moment, she shuddered.

She had just heard a voice that was strangely like that of her late father.

But Betty calmed her, telling her she was merely under the influence of an illusion.

She was finally beginning to recover her composure when the so-called professor came in, and, as she hadn't ever seen him before, she seemed terrified by this frightening figure that had been described to her.

But the "professor" hastened to remove his false teeth and mask, and it revealed the face of none other than Burke, for the "transfer of power", so to speak, had just taken place in the hallway.

"Yes, it's me," said the detective, "and all this is part of our plan. Look at me, Lucile, look me in the eye. I'm going to ask you to allow me to put you into the state in which you were in five years ago. You won't feel any pain or discomfort. Relax completely and don't resist."

And once again the detective began applying magnetic touches to the young woman's face; these produced their effect quickly, for the young woman, passive and unaware of her surroundings, accepted all of the suggestions made to her under hypnosis.

He didn't put her to sleep, and she remained in a receptive state, submissive but awake.

"This is good work," he said when he had finished, "let's now go and see Sir Roger Bradford."

He went into the next room and found himself face to face with an honourable gentleman who was drinking glasses of whiskey and smoking cigarettes while waiting for events to take their course.

"Very good!" said Burke, "you are an authentic Roger Bradford and now, remember that Sir Roger's voice was even deeper than yours, especially when he spoke loudly."

"So will I have to say a lot?" asked the fake Roger Bradford.

"No, it would be pointless, because the people who are now about to perform in your company will hear only the voice that spoke to them five years ago; all you'll have to do is move your lips, which is most fortunate, because I wasn't there when Sir Roger greeted his killer, and therefore I can't tell you what he said to that person."

* * *

At that moment the doorbell rang.

The detective quickly reinserted his false teeth and readjusted his mask, and, with a brief signal, ordered all present to take up their positions.

"The ceremony is about to begin," he said. "Bradford, go to your study. Sit down at the desk and pretend to be writing."

Then, turning towards Bryce: "And you, go see who's at the door and admit whoever it is."

And going into the next room, he found Betty and told her: "Go and fetch Williams, who is still in Sir James' house, and tell him I need him to come here and reoccupy the bedroom that was his five years ago. You mustn't leave him alone for a single second. He's the only one I didn't think it necessary to hypnotize and I have my own reasons for that."

Betty left without a word. In her present role, a simple nod of the head on her part signified that she had understood.

Luna was still with Lucile.

"And you, Luna," said Burke, "you may now allow Lady Lucile to do as she will. You will simply stay ready in the room adjoining Sir Roger's study and Bryce will join you there…Bryce, who was that at the door?"

This question had been triggered by the arrival of the inspector, Bryce, who needed to have a word with his chief, Detective Burke. The latter had, moreover, guessed what he had come to say.

"I opened the door," said Bryce.

"And it was Sir James who presented himself," replied the detective, finishing the sentence.

"Yes."

"What did he ask you?"

"He's asking for Sir Roger Bradford. He wishes to speak to him in person."

"Good, and what answer did you give him?"

"I asked him to wait, but he doesn't seem to understand; I presume that in the past he always used to be brought in to see his cousin without having to be formally announced."

"So, quickly, show him into the study."

And, while Bryce was running to show Sir James into the study, Burke went, in his turn, into that fatal room by a different door.

He hid himself in a corner of the room, behind the curtains that he now drew fully in order to completely conceal himself, and, having made a sign with a nod of his head to "Roger Bradford", who was sitting comfortably in an armchair, he waited.

At almost that very same instant, Sir James came into the room.

He immediately made his way to where his cousin was sitting and offered a handshake, which the actor returned, his lips moving as he muttered several indistinct words.

Sir James didn't at all hear this present-day voice but rather, that voice from beyond the grave that now crossed time and space to resound once again in his ears.

He listened to the fake Roger Bradford and, finally, bowed his head while a smile lit up his face.

And he replied to the question that he had been asked five years previously.

"That's very kind of you, Roger, I'm extremely touched that you want me to be the executor of your will. Although, in reality, you still have plenty of time to think about those kinds of matters!"

He waited for about another thirty seconds as the sham Roger Bradford merely moved his lips. Sir James then went on:

"Yes, of course, I understand it gives you great peace of mind to know that, if anything were to happen to you, I would become Lucile's guardian."

And then, in a perfectly natural way, he moved closer to the actor and as soon as he was right beside him, he placed his hand on his shoulder.

This position in which he was now standing offered one significant advantage to Burke: it allowed him to see Sir James' face directly opposite him, whereas up to that moment the hypnotized gentleman had had his back half turned away from him.

And, on that face, Burke suddenly saw a significant transition taking place.

The usual vague, abstracted expression of Roger Bradford's cousin's face was imperceptibly shifting to something quite different, while his eyes were moving, to become intently fixed on the door opposite the desk. The actor who was playing the part of the dead man was at a loss to know what to do next, and Burke himself also felt quite awkward, as he didn't know what to think, when the door suddenly opened and Lucile appeared.

The young woman said:

"Father, if you need me, I'm in the small drawing room with Arthur; we're playing a little bit of music; I hope it doesn't disturb you."

The actor passing himself off as Roger Bradford replied with a mechanical shake of his head to indicate that it wouldn't disturb him at all, and Lucile smiled sweetly at him.

"Good God!" murmured Burke, "I'd really like to know what that famous Hibbs is getting up to right now."

But at that moment, from the other side of the wall, a voice reached his ears:

"Don't worry, I'm keeping watch over him."

This reply reassured Burke. It was Bryce who had just spoken.

Lucile had answered her father with a smile, greeted Sir James with a gracious bow, and had then gone out, softly closing the door behind her.

Then, after a moment's silence, Sir James spoke.

"Lucile is truly a delightful person, Roger, and, do you know what touches me more than anything else in the decision you've just made? It's that I have high hopes of her one day becoming my wife."

When the cousin had finished speaking thus, Sir Roger's impersonator jumped as though in shock and looked at him, and this wordless cue was so adept that it influenced Sir James himself, so that he recoiled slightly, probably because his cousin, five years earlier, had similarly started in disbelief.

But Sir Roger, five years previously, had really spoken, and Burke soon discovered what he had said, by a process of deduction, based on the reply now given by Sir James:

"Obviously she's only a child and marriage is out of the question for the moment, but in five or six years' time she shall be old enough to be my wife…What? What are you saying? I'll be fifty-two years of age by then… and what of it?…That baronet of yours who was such a frequent visitor to your home up to recently, no doubt hoping himself to marry Lucile, was three years older than me…"

Silence once again.

"Yes," Sir James went on, "I know, you banished him from your house…What? You will banish me too, if I insist…no, you won't do that…"

He was panting, his hands were moving feverishly and he was banging on the desk with his fist.

Suddenly, he lowered his voice and turned to look at the door but, as there was no sign of anybody about to come in, he continued, speaking now in a lower voice than before.

"What are you saying now? That I frittered away part of your fortune and that if I insist, you'll make me leave for good…And you'll then leave Lucile under my nephew's guardianship…"

Sir James approached the actor as if he was going to grab him by the shoulders; but he checked himself; his arms were back at his side once more, and there was now a look of panic in his eyes.

"No," he stammered, "no…you shall not treat me so cruelly, you shall not banish me from this house. I'm not a thief, as you are well aware, and I want Lucile for I love her with all my heart and soul; she's not going to become any other man's wife, I'll see to that – even if I have to…"

He stopped abruptly; his face lit up with an evil smile and chuckling, and, with frantic, impulsive speed, he opened the desk drawer, the small drawer on the right that was there directly in front of him since he was standing beside Sir Roger; and, thrusting his hand inside, he took a revolver out from it and, immediately, held the barrel of the gun against the actor's temple.

The latter – despite being well-prepared for the inevitable conclusion of this dramatic scene – now looked, with a desperate appeal in his eyes, towards the corner where Burke stood concealed from view by the double curtains.

Unquestionably there was no bullet in that weapon kept in Sir Roger's desk drawer, but even if there was only powder in the chamber, its lethal effect would be practically the same, and the actor would certainly be killed by the discharge.

But, from behind the curtains, the detective made a sign to reassure him.

Burke listened attentively to every single word uttered by Sir James, not missing anything. The latter was now holding the barrel of the revolver against his cousin's forehead as he said:

"I hate you, Roger, do you hear me? Your whole life, you've treated me like the black sheep of the family, all because I had my own ideas, because I wanted to live a different life from the one you lead. And now that I love your daughter, and am willing to do everything I can to make her happy, you continue to make me live in a state of constant suffering. Well, no! I don't intend to continue suffering until my dying day. It's over. I have you now, and I won't let you escape. I want to live, and to live happily; to break free from your control. Take this piece of paper, and write down what I tell you."

And he began to dictate: there was unmistakeable madness in the gleam of his eyes, yet his voice was distinct:

Lucile,

I have decided, of my own volition, to kill myself; forgive me for the pain that I'm about to cause you.

And, almost immediately, he pulled the trigger; there was only a muffled sound, but, at the same time, a bang reverberated.

It was the detective, who had emptied a bullet from his own revolver into the floor.

Emerging from his hiding place, he rushed into the hallway and, from the foot of the stairs, "Betty, did you hear that?"

And, from the third-floor landing, Betty's voice replied:

"Yes; Williams and I both heard it."

"Perfect," Burke went on. "Send Williams down to me."

There was then the sound of someone rushing, almost tumbling, down the stairs, and Williams came to a halt on the ground floor, followed by Betty Adams.

"So there you have it: that superior, supernatural force that impelled you to come downstairs," said the detective. "The truth is that, on the day of Sir Roger's death, you heard the gunshot. Now, come into the study and stay beside me."

Williams obeyed without protest, saying nothing to defend himself.

In the study, the final episode of that fateful scene was being re-enacted in the manner in which, five years previously, it had undoubtedly unfolded. The fake Roger Bradford lay on the carpet while Sir James, who had just watched his victim collapsing onto the floor, leant over him and quietly placed the revolver in his hand.

He then turned towards Williams, who was standing at the other end of the room. And he spoke:

"Williams, as you have seen, your master has committed suicide."

The butler turned to the detective.

"What should I reply?" he asked.

"Exactly as you replied five years ago."

"No," replied Williams with a shudder, "I won't do it."

Burke shrugged his shoulders. "In that case I'll do it for you. Here is what you said, more or less – I'm practically certain."

And turning towards the killer, he said:

"Sir James, my master did not kill himself, but as I have been in the service of this house for so long and know that a scandal would forevermore destroy the family's reputation, I shall say nothing."

Williams hung his head. This was exactly the gist of what he had replied.

And, as though Sir James had indeed heard Williams replying to him with those words, he went towards the butler, saying:

"I know, Williams, that you have lent significant amounts of money to my cousin; rest assured that every last penny shall be repaid to you, and I'll even pay you more."

The detective then grasped Williams by the shoulder, and leading him out of the study, pushed him, so to speak, into Betty's arms, saying to her:

"Arrest him, Miss Adams! And advise him that anything he says from this moment onwards may be used against him in a court of law."

IV

What Arthur Hibbs Had Been Doing All This Time

VERY QUICKLY AFTER the above arrest, Sir James looked round the room with visible terror in his eyes, and, getting up from the seat in which Burke had made him sit, he asked: "What has happened?"

"Nothing that wasn't completely expected," the detective replied. "But I'm arresting you in the name of His Majesty the King, and must advise you that anything you say from this moment onwards may be used against you in a court of law."

Sir James didn't make any movement; he was looking at the body of the actor spread-eagled across the wooden floor.

Burke didn't intend to take any further advantage of purely theatrical effects just to give Sir James a lesson in morality, which would have been pointless. So he ordered Sir Roger Bradford's impersonator: "Get up."

Then, turning towards the accused man, he said: "This man, as you can now see for yourself, isn't your cousin; but it was you who committed the murder that, five years ago, enabled you to rid yourself of Sir Roger. Do you have anything to say?"

Sir James made no reply.

Burke then called Williams, who came forward, handcuffed.

"Here is Sir Roger's butler," Burke continued. "Williams has not been hypnotized by me. I needed a witness who was guided only by his own conscience. Williams, can you now confirm to Sir James that you haven't been pressurized by me in any way whatsoever, nor subjected to any kind of treatment that would have been against the law?"

Williams replied simply: "I acknowledge that this is the truth of the matter."

"Good. Will you therefore speak truthfully and say what it was you saw five years ago when you came into the drawing room, your attention having been attracted by the gunshot?"

Williams, without looking at Sir James, stated: "I shall tell the whole truth…"

And he described how he had seen Sir James placing the revolver into his master's hand, and what he had said at that moment, and also what had been promised to him.

"And now, Sir James," said Burke, "that's where we are at, right now. What do you intend to do? Do you still maintain that Sir Roger committed suicide, or do you finally admit to having killed him in a moment of madness because he had refused you Lucile's hand in marriage and was threatening to banish you forever from his home?"

The accused man hung his head. Burke waited a few moments and then went on:

"Do you wish me to take your silence as an admission of guilt?"

Sir James nodded his head in confirmation.

The detective then turned to the people who had witnessed this scene:

"You have seen and heard what has just taken place," he said. "Sir James admits to being Sir Roger's killer. Betty, I'm going to ask you to be kind enough to call the three inspectors who are in the garden so that they can take care of our prisoners. As for me, I'm going to go see what Bryce is doing."

And just as he was leaving the room, he turned towards Betty:

"Ah! Another thing – tell the inspectors not to go away, for there will perhaps be another arrest."

As soon as he was in the front room, Burke called out: "Where are you, Bryce?"

The inspector's voice replied:

"In the small drawing room, Sir; can you come and join me, please?"

The small drawing room in which the manor's residents ordinarily gathered to sing and play the piano, was on the first floor of the residence.

When he went into that room, the detective saw that Arthur and Lucile were seated side by side and were holding hands.

"What happened?" Burke asked the inspector.

And the latter recounted the scene he had just witnessed, displaying the characteristic clarity and perfection that he put into all his official reports.

"Well, it's like this. First of all, Lady Lucile sat down at the piano" - he pointed to the old piano that, for a long time, had no longer contained any cords - "and began to play. Shortly afterwards, Mr. Hibbs came into the room and, softly approaching Lucile, kissed her neck. She straightened up, startled, and they began to talk. Lady Lucile roundly reproached Mr. Hibbs, telling him he had no right to behave in this manner and that he must go away. However, following Mr Hibbs' insistence, she agreed to listen to what he had to say and it was at that moment that she went downstairs to let her father know where she would be if he needed her. While she was out of the room, Mr. Hibbs went to the window and, rapping his fingers on the pane, murmured: 'Sir Roger will never agree, because I am without any fortune of my own.' Lady Lucile came back upstairs; they then rushed into each other's arms, and the young woman said: 'I can never live without you, Arthur.' After which they went on to do all that young lovers usually do in such situations, and kissed each other several times. It was then that the sound of the gunshot in the study was heard.

"Lucile wanted to rush downstairs immediately, convinced that something terrible must have happened. She was troubled, indeed terrified. Mr. Hibbs then managed to calm her down, telling her that it was nothing, probably one of the servants amusing himself by shooting crows in the garden. He even said that such gunfire was a regular occurrence each evening, and Lady Lucile seemed to take his word for it. However, at a certain point, their attention was drawn to the sound of the commotion on the ground floor and the young woman even said, a few times: 'Did you hear that? Doors are being slammed!'

"Hibbs then appeared troubled and he went out onto the landing to listen. When he came back into the room to speak to Lucile once again, he was a little pale. 'I don't think it's anything serious,' he said, 'but all the same, I think I'll go back home just to let my uncle know.'

"And he would have gone out of the house if I hadn't taken the precaution of locking the doors. That's where we're at, Sir, at present."

"So," asked Burke, "are the young people still in the small drawing room?"

"Yes," replied Bryce.

Burke went into the drawing room and asked Bryce to stay in the hall.

He wished to question Arthur without any witnesses present.

However, as soon as he saw the two young people, he didn't have the heart to ask Lucile to leave the room, and Mr. Hibbs' current manner gave him to believe that he would easily obtain whatever information he wished; the young man seemed extremely downhearted and, sprawled in an armchair, was evidently drained.

The detective began by reviving the young man and set about making him fully conscious of his acts.

"Forgive me, Mr. Hibbs," he said, "I have mistreated you somewhat, but it was absolutely necessary to do so. We still have a few small points to clear up but, before we get to those, allow me to inform you that Sir Roger's killer has confessed to his crime."

Arthur straightened himself in his chair, then, standing up, staring at Mr. Burke, he spat out the sarcastic, bitter comment:

"So it wasn't *you*, after all?"

"It was Sir James," replied Burke after a brief hesitation.

He was watching Mr. Hibbs' reaction closely; the latter manifested such sincere astonishment and seemed so genuinely staggered at this revelation, that the detective realized the young man had never once suspected his uncle.

Arthur had got such a devastating shock that, despite his best efforts, he was forced to hold onto the old piano to stop himself from falling down, so stunned was he.

"Sir James! Can it be possible?"

And because Lucile herself – speechless, paralyzed, and so pale that she looked about to faint – was on the point of asking Burke to explain himself regarding this accusation, the latter went on:

"Yes, it's Sir James, and he has just confessed to his crime. Just before his confession, he had recreated, before my very eyes, the scene of the murder, exactly as it had unfolded five years ago; and unable to keep up the pretence any longer, he then stated that he was indeed the murderer."

It was obvious that Lucile would be unable to listen to any more of this, and that her peace of mind would have been seriously jeopardized if she were subjected to too long an ordeal.

Burke thus decided to have her brought back to the neighbouring dwelling; and Betty, who had by now been relieved of her duty of watching over the arrested killer thanks to the arrival of reinforcements in the shape of three additional inspectors, led her mistress back to the house next door.

The detective was now free to speak to Arthur with complete openness, and the young man also recounted the thoughts that had gone through his mind on the day of the tragedy.

After hearing the sound of the gunshot, he had gone back to his own house.

"Because," he explained, "I didn't want to be found alone with Lucile in the drawing room. Obviously I had no idea that Sir Roger had been killed, but I feared that the sound of gunfire had plunged the house into turmoil and that I was likely to be discovered at any moment. I therefore returned home, and, in order to make it look as though I was perfectly composed, I took a book and pretended to be reading. I had been in my room for about a quarter of an hour when Sir James appeared and cried out to me: 'Sir Roger has just killed himself; quickly, come with me!'

"I wasn't surprised at the fact that my uncle had already learned of the death, because he had left the house for a short time following a rather unpleasant argument with me about Lucile, to go to his cousin's place. I got him to briefly explain the circumstances of the tragedy to me and, about ten minutes later, I was going into Sir Roger's house with him and I was really astonished, I must admit, to see that you were already at the scene of the crime, and standing over the dead body. I couldn't believe for one moment that Sir Roger could possibly have committed suicide."

"Why not?" asked Burke.

"Because he simply wasn't the kind of man who decides to take his own life. He was a fighter, a man who, in the face of adversity, gives the impression that he would keep on fighting to the very end, and most of all because he loved his daughter very deeply. Therefore, from that moment, I was convinced that Sir Roger had been murdered."

And Burke looked at him carefully.

"So, when you saw me standing over the body, you believed that *I* was the killer?"

"Yes," Arthur candidly admitted. "Tell me the truth: how could you have got to Sir Roger's house so quickly after he was killed?"

Burke smiled.

"Because," he murmured, "I was already there *before* the murder had even been committed!"

Arthur seemed astounded. "You were at Sir Roger's house!" he exclaimed, "and we weren't even aware of it! You must admit, that's very strange!"

"And yet it's the truth. Sir Roger had phoned me that afternoon and asked me to call to see him, to tell me about certain strange things he had recently discovered. The day before, he had actually received a death threat from an anonymous phone caller. The caller had told him that his daughter Lucile would be kidnapped and held hostage if he didn't agree to give her hand in marriage, immediately, to whoever requested it."

At that moment, there came a knock on the door and a voice in the hall asked:

"Sir, what are we to do with the prisoners? Should we take them away? The police car has been phoned for and the police officers are outside in the street."

Burke quickly gave Arthur permission to leave, telling him he would see him later, and went back down to the study.

Sir James, like a hunted animal, had taken refuge behind the inspectors and, his hands bound, was maintaining a fierce silence.

The detective walked directly up to where he stood.

"Sir James," he said, "I'm going to ask you only one question. Earlier this evening, you tried to kill your nephew in his bedroom; don't try to deny it because, when you opened the door halfway to fire the shot, I saw the ring gleaming on your finger, as the light from the hall struck it from the side. Tell me why you wished to commit that murder: because Mr. Hibbs was in love with Lucile, isn't that it?"

A sardonic smile creased the killer's lips.

"It wasn't my nephew I was trying to finish off tonight," he murmured. "It was *you*."

"Me!"

"Yes! Because I'd been watching his room while you were having a cigar with him, and I knew that you hadn't gone back to your own bedroom. When I opened the door, I saw that he was lying down on the sofa and therefore, it could only be you who was lying on the actual bed. So I fired; and unfortunately, I missed you."

"Well!" said Burke, "I can't blame you too much for doing so, Sir James. After all, it was all part and parcel of your defense system. You shall be charged with murder, and attempted murder; that will be the whole of it."

He was just about to give the order for Sir James to be taken into custody, when the latter made a request.

"I would like," he asked, "to remain alone here for one moment with you. Will you grant me that favour?"

"Why not?" replied Burke.

He asked the police officers to leave the two of them alone and then, when he was alone with Sir James, instead of asking him what he had to say, he took a revolver out of his pocket and placed it on the desk, very near to where the accused man was standing.

"Be careful; don't touch it whatever you do; this gun is loaded!"

Then he made as if to walk towards the door leading out onto the hall and, without looking at Sir James, he said, in a low voice:

"I have to give an order to Bryce; excuse me for one second."

But he had hardly taken a step out of the study when a loud bang was heard and the detective, pushing the door that he hadn't even had time to close, saw Sir James collapsed in front of the desk, still holding in his tied hands the revolver he had taken from the table. He had put the gun to his forehead and shot himself.

"This isn't really following the rule book," murmured Burke, "but I'm certain that nobody in the family will think any the worse of me."

V

In Which Mr. Burke Finds Himself Accused

"MR. BURKE," began the Chief Magistrate of the official police, "I have asked you to come here today so that we can come to a mutual understanding about this whole business."

The Chief Magistrate's tone was severe and grave, but Mr. Burke didn't seem to be worried about it.

"I'm listening, Sir."

"Mr. Burke," the Chief Magistrate continued, "you have investigated the Sir Roger Bradford murder case outside the aegis of the official police force; and in doing so, you've made use of certain methods for which you've already been severely reprimanded."

Burke looked up in astonishment.

"And haven't I been successful in solving that case?" he asked.

"Admittedly, you were successful; indeed, one could even say that you were *too* successful, seeing that by once again exceeding the leeway allowed to you by the law you have facilitated the suicide of the murderer."

He was about to continue, once again seeming to put the detective on trial for his particular use of hypnotism, when Burke stood up.

"Please allow me," he said, "to ask two people to sit in on this discussion – two people whom I asked to come here today and who are probably waiting in the room adjoining your office."

And, opening the door himself, he asked the Court Usher to show in the visitors who were indeed waiting.

Lucile and Arthur came into the office.

As soon as introductions had been made, Mr. Burke continued speaking.

"It was my wish," he said, "that the people most closely involved and interested in this case should be here to listen to my explanations, as given now to the senior legal authority that you represent, Sir."

He paused and remained silent for a moment, his chin resting on his joined hands.

"I was in Sir Roger's house the night he was killed, but, as I was in my bedroom at the precise moment of his death, I had no way of knowing how the murder had taken place. One thing was, however, obvious: that the killer was somebody well-known to the members of the household; the statements made by the servants were positive on that point, that nobody else had come into the house…I pretended to reach a conclusion of suicide, and left. But, even while I was occupied with other criminal cases, I continuously thought about this one. As you know, Detective Burke isn't ever the kind of man who leaves a mystery unsolved! It was obvious that the murderer would not confess to his crime unless he were forced to do so, and somehow subdued, as it were. But how could those ends be achieved? What needed to be done? In a nutshell, he would have to be put in a state of mind in which he would be absolutely incapable of controlling his own actions. It was then that I set about 'resurrecting' Sir Roger. It took me a certain amount of time to find an actor who could play that part. But I found him in the person of an excellent music-hall performer, accustomed to acting and to wearing disguises and costumes, a performer who, with his variety-show partner Luna, became my associate over the course of a few days. The solution lay in making a strong impact on imagination! Human beings who have committed a serious wrongdoing are always more or less susceptible to remorse. Even when they haven't confessed, their crime continues to weigh heavily on their conscience, and that situation makes them extremely receptive to suggestions made to them under hypnosis. Inspector Bryce was entrusted with the mission of playing the part of the mysterious new tenant, and I managed to find him a disguise perfectly apt to strike terror into the hearts of any living beings who might be in any way impressionable!"

The Chief Magistrate murmured:

"Neither is that very…very…"

Burke ignored this half-formulated criticism.

"I will dare to say," he continued, "that Inspector Bryce managed to make himself look like a creature who was very likely to terrorize and horrify all who saw him! So, we immediately created the scenario of the so-called vampires; your household was certainly subjected to a very rough campaign of terror, Mr. Hibbs. You must admit, you seemed to be surrounded by supernatural beings! You came to be influenced by them. Betty, the very worthy assistant whom I trained myself, played the part of a terrified servant to perfection. It was she who planted that book on vampires that you read, Mr. Hibbs, in your personal collection. It was also she who rummaged about in your sofa and who found the notes that you had taken on the investigation, concerning your suspicions of me."

Arthur didn't say a word; he had taken Lucile's hand and was holding it tightly.

"You must admit," Mr. Burke continued, "that the way you behaved towards me could be construed by me as suspicious. I thought for a while that I was making you feel ill-at-ease and that you were seeking to somehow get ahead of me. Didn't you yourself try to get me to believe in demonic forces, vampires, ghosts and all other imaginable supernatural creatures?"

Arthur replied:

"I wanted to test you on that subject: if you had blamed the murder on vampires, my mind would have been made up."

"I didn't realize that until later," Burke went on, "and I then proceeded to study your uncle's character in depth. I led him to believe that Sir Roger was still alive, and even gave him 'proof' that this was so."

Arthur jumped up from his seat, suddenly struck by a thought.

"But, in actual fact," he exclaimed, "didn't my uncle assure me that Sir Roger's body was no longer in its tomb? It was from that moment onwards that he appeared to have become unhinged by the succession of events that caused such upheaval in our lives. Did you, by any chance, remove Sir Roger's corpse, Mr. Burke?"

The detective smiled.

"No, Mr. Hibbs…"

The Chief Magistrate sighed with relief. He was, indeed, very glad that Burke hadn't contravened the excessive prohibitions of British law in such a macabre fashion.

"I don't suffer from necrophagia," Burke went on, "that is, I'm not in the habit of feeding on dead bodies! I simply confined myself to lightly lifting the lid of the coffin, and I was the only one to look into it that night because Sir James, in a state of extreme distress, remained standing at the door of the tomb."

Arthur cried out:

"So Sir Roger hadn't somehow risen from his coffin!"

"Of course not! Except that I told Sir James he was no longer inside his tomb, and he didn't ask to see for himself; he took my word for it, and thereby made a fatal error."

"But why," asked Lucile, "did you act upon Sir James rather than anybody else? After all, he was the one who called you."

"Let me remind you that he called on me in order to protect himself from the strangers who were living next door, not for me to conduct an investigation into Sir Roger's death. He was so sure that he had gotten away with his crime and could never possibly be found out, he so strongly presumed that the case had been permanently closed, that he had sold the bearer securities that had gone missing from Sir Roger's desk. Admittedly, that wasn't proof of murder, since he was Lady Lucile's guardian, but it could hardly be considered as arguing in favour of his innocence."

The Chief Magistrate was listening to the detective with visible interest, and he was beginning to regret that the police force was now deprived of the services of a man of such high competence. There could no longer be any question of reprimanding or admonishing him, and the magistrate followed the discussion with keen professional interest and as if he himself had been closely involved in it. Seeing that Mr. Burke had stopped speaking for a moment in order to try to recall specific details, he took the opportunity of asking him a question.

"You are aware," he said, "that we still have a certain Williams Haynes, the victim's butler, in custody. He is accused of being an accomplice to the crime; do you still intend to prosecute him? You know that he has withdrawn his previous statements and that he now maintains categorically that he never heard the revolver being fired that night."

Lucile, speaking before Burke got a chance to reply, immediately interjected:

"Sir, Williams certainly bears no guilt in this matter; I'm convinced that he acted only out of kindness towards me."

"But Williams is most certainly guilty in the eyes of the law, as he didn't give truthful evidence from the start, contrary to the requirements of the justice system, and a charge of complicity could certainly be made against him," said Burke.

The Chief Magistrate agreed.

"Clearly that is so," he said. "And yet…"

He left his unfinished sentence hanging in the air, not revealing his true intentions, wondering what the detective was going to say next.

Burke realized that he would perhaps have less difficulty than he had imagined in scoring a further victory.

"I think," he went on, speaking more and more slowly, as though carefully weighing his words, "that we should have the case against Williams dismissed, because, in actual fact, I'm the only one who knows about his confession, and everything he has said since then has been a categorical and formal retraction."

The Chief Magistrate nodded.

"And yet it's hardly standard practice," he murmured.

"If we were always obliged to take account of correct legal procedures," said Burke slowly, "we wouldn't get very far when it comes to catching criminals. For those fellows have their own ways and means that manage to circumvent the letter of the law."

It didn't seem as though Burke had anything more to say, nor even as if Mr. Hibbs or Lucile had anything further to ask him.

The young man, his mind buzzing with deep thoughts, remained in his seat, and it had to be pointed out to him that the discussion had ended, before he stood up.

When he finally saw that Burke was standing, he himself got ready to leave; but before going out, he turned towards the Chief Magistrate.

"Sir," he said, "I overheard what you said earlier to Mr. Burke about his investigation. I wouldn't want you to believe for one moment that any of us have any fault to find with him. In a word, I believe I'm also speaking for Lucile when I offer my thanks to Mr. Burke in your presence and assure him that we will always remember him fondly and with deep gratitude."

Then, turning towards the detective, he said: "Sir, would you like to come and have dinner with us tomorrow evening?"

* * *

The unhappiest person at the conclusion of this case was undoubtedly Harris.

At first, the Welshman hadn't wanted to believe that Betty had played so important a role in Sir James' house. When he realized that she had really belonged to such a respectable British institution as the official Police force, he remained speechless for at least half a day, only recovering his voice when he had gone looking for it at the bottom of a bottle of whiskey. What could he hope for now, as far as his love life was concerned? Clearly not a great deal.

When the former cook returned to the house to collect some clothes she'd left there, he could hardly dare to even greet her, and he blushed like a young woman.

Betty was most gracious with him, telling him that if he ever needed her services as a police officer, she would be at his disposal. Betty had only joined the police force after this investigation, but she was already in a position to exercise some influence there.

But Harris looked at her sorrowfully and shook his head.

"In my family," he said, "we don't kill each other, and the only thing anybody has ever stolen from me is a sixpenny coin I'd tied round my neck on the end of a string when I was twelve."

"Well," asked Betty, "do you want me to help you find the person who stole your sixpenny coin?"

Harris declined her offer.

He was almost as afraid of detectives as of thieves, and when he reflected on the fact that he had lived with this kind person for so long without for one moment suspecting the functions she had been secretly exercising, he still shuddered.

"No," he said, "please don't take care of anything at all for me, but if I've ever said anything unpleasant to you, Miss Betty, you'll have to forgive me, and if I ever chanced to dishonour people I know by telling you they'd done this or that to me, you must try to forget their names… because I would be angry if there were still vampires because of me!"

And this exchange ended with a hearty handshake; from then onwards, there was no longer any question of romance between Betty and Harris.

The murder of Sir Roger Bradford was known only to a few rare individuals who happened to be acquainted with the case, and there was nothing about it in the newspapers. That is why you would never have known a thing about it if we hadn't narrated it in complete detail, for the greater glory of Mr. Burke, of whom we will perhaps speak to you again one day.

THE END

BOISYVON.

Translated by Kieran O'Driscoll, Dublin, Ireland. September, 2017
kieran.odriscoll3@mail.dcu.ie
Linked In: Kieran O'Driscoll.
Edited by Thomas Mann

Afterword

As mentioned in the Preface, and as discussed in detail in *London After Midnight: A New Reconstruction Based on Contemporary Sources* (BearManor Media, 2016), the best record we have of what was actually in now-lost film is provided by its cutting continuity. This is an unpublished typescript compiled by the film's editor Harry Reynolds working with director Tod Browning; it is an unillustrated, skeletal list of all of the individual screen shots in the released version of the film, specifying in each the actors, the stage directions for their activities, and their dialogue as given in the intertitles written by Joe Farnham. It also indicates camera positionings (e.g., close-up, medium shot, long shot, etc.).[1] Again, the plot of the story as given in that continuity is substantially different from that found in the Waldemar Young shooting script for the film (under the title "The Hypnotist"), the contemporary Marie Coolidge-Rask novelization of that script, and the pressbook of publicity material. Further, the "final" plot represented in the continuity itself is noticeably incoherent. The evidence presented in my previous book indicates, however, that the script, the novel, and the pressbook were available to the author of the 1928 British *Boy's Cinema* fictionization of the story, and that he used them to fill in many of the plot gaps he saw on the screen. The author of *Londres Après Minuit*, however, evidently did not have access to these English language supplemental materials; he had to make up the necessary "filler" material entirely from his own imagination. And so

---

1. A copy of this document is recorded as "London After Midnight, Cutting Continuity, November 25, 1927, Library of Congress copyright documentation, LP25289m Motion Picture Broadcasting/Recorded Sound Division" and is held at the Library's facility in Culpeper, Virginia. It is still under copyright protection until 2022 and cannot be published until then, although "fair use" quotations may be made from it.

even though both the British and the French fictionizations were based on viewings of the same film, and both follow its basic plot line, they nonetheless provide two significantly different variants of the film story.

The novel by Lucien Boisyvon makes minor changes to the names of several characters. The murder victim Roger Balfour in the continuity becomes Roger Bradford; his daughter Lucille (with two "l"s) becomes Lucile (with one). The gardener in the novel is given the name "Harris" while in the continuity he remains nameless. When the maid is referred to in the latter she is designated either "Miss Smithson" or "Polly Moran" (the actress who played her); in the novel, she is "Betty" or "Betty Adams". In the continuity this character is referred to as a maid while in the novel she is usually designated the cook (although Burke, in the novel, also once refers to her as "your maid" [*votre bonne*]). The vampiric character is referred to in the continuity as either "Burke", "Chaney", or (in one sequence) the "old man" when Chaney is in the make-up; when his assistant detective wears the cape and teeth in other scenes he is referred to as "the vampire" or "the stranger". In the novel the vampire character is referred to simply by his self-designation as "the professor"; the description of him given there is that his "ghastly white complexion was not at all that of living human beings," and "From his gums, constantly exposed to view, emerged two rows of sparkling teeth that gave his face a ferocious expression. One's eyes were constantly drawn to this bizarre set of teeth." This is a good literary description of Lon Chaney's makeup; the novel, however, adds a detail not mentioned in the continuity, that the character is frequently heard to be "chuckling" with a "strange, silent, sarcastic little laugh."

Most of the differences between the continuity and the novel appear in the plot. For the sake of brevity in what follows I will refer to the details given in the former as being those of either "the film itself" *or* "the continuity"; and to those in the present translation as being in "the French novel" or simply "the novel." References to the translation are to its subsections, e.g., "Part One, Chapter Three" will be indicated as (1.III). I will also sometimes abbreviate references to the cutting continuity as the **CC**, and those to the French novel as **FrN**.

The author of the novel simply ignores, to begin with, a contradiction appearing early on in the film, as to whether the story takes place in London itself or in one of its suburban areas (i.e., the **CC** begins with a 'Fade In' to the intertitle "Roger Balfour was found dead in his London home" but shortly afterward shows the real estate agent, via an intertitle, offering to drive the vampire character "back to London" after completing the lease transaction for the same house in which the murder took place). The locale in the French novel is never at issue.

The novel is inconsistent on the family status of Arthur Hibbs: In **FrN1.I** Sir James (himself a cousin to the deceased Sir Roger) refers to him as "my nephew", and elsewhere in the narrative that term is used repeatedly to designate him. Indeed, this is how he is referred to in the film itself, which the novelist was following. In **FrN1.V**, however, Lucile tells Burke that Hibbs is, in relation to herself, a "*very distant* cousin. In actual fact, *I don't think we're even related*, but as *he was adopted by Sir James*, I consider him my cousin" [emphasis added]. This is a detail not in the film. It is apparently necessitated from the fact that the novelist, to account for the close connection of the households of Sir Roger and Sir James, makes those two gentlemen to be cousins to begin with. In the film, however, they are simply unrelated friends (the **CC** having Sir James refer to the decedent as "my friend Balfour"); and the **CC** gives no justification for the intimacy of the two households other than that their inhabitants are apparently long-time friendly neighbors. At the end of the **CC** Burke, in addressing Arthur, refers to Lucille as "your reward" just before the two go off together – a sequence that suggests that the couple will go on to spend their lives with each other. The French novelist, in adding his own detail of the *distance* of their family connection, seems concerned to indicate that their eventual union will not be one of a too-close blood relationship, a problem that does not arise in the film.

Elsewhere the French author again initially follows the film closely in having the butler Williams tell Detective Burke that he, Williams, did not hear the shot that killed his master, Sir Roger, but that "some strange, supernatural force drove me to make my way down here" (**FrN 1.I**; **CC**: "Some strange unnatural power urged me to come and see if Mr. Balfour was all right.") Later developments in the novel, however, tell us that Williams did indeed hear the shot, and that he came immediately to the murder site and witnessed Sir James putting the gun into the deceased Sir Roger's hand (2.IV). This plot line is not in the film.

Detective Burke's appearance at the scene of Sir Roger's murder

The same sequence in the novel is muddled, however, by the way in which its author deals with another problem in the film: the fact that, in the **CC**, Detective Burke appears at the crime scene only a few minutes after the shooting. Young Hibbs directly challenges him on this – in both the **CC** and the **FrN**:

> **CC:** "If he has been dead only fifteen minutes…how did you get here so soon?"

> **FrN:** "If he died half an hour ago, how come you are already here? Might you, by chance, have been present when Sir Roger was killed?"

In the film, Burke gives no explanation at all for his early arrival, and in a rather bullying manner he simply snaps at Hibbs peremptorily saying "That's my business, young man!" In the novel, he shows no such anger at the challenge, and essentially sidesteps the question without answering it. In the latter source, however, we find later that Burke was indeed already in Sir James' house at the time of the shooting – a circumstance not in the film:

> **FrN2.IV:** [Burke]: "I was already there before the murder had even been committed!"…"And yet it's the truth. Sir Roger had phoned me that afternoon and asked me to call to see him, to tell me about certain strange things he had recently discovered. The day before, he had actually received a death threat from an anonymous phone caller. The caller had told him that his daughter Lucile would be kidnapped and held hostage if he didn't agree to give her hand in marriage, immediately, to whoever requested it."

This explanation (given by Burke as to *why* he was present in the house at the time of the murder) is also not in the film; and it creates an unnecessary distraction in the reader's mind because it is so implausible: why would anyone demand Sir Roger's daughter by means of a combined threat of kidnapping or death when the beneficiary of the demand – the one to marry Lucile – must then patently be connected to, if not exactly identifiable with, the maker of the demand? Making a threat with this intended outcome provides no way for its source to remain "anonymous" for long; it simple beggars credibility.

The novelist's proffering of this explanation for Burke's presence at the murder scene, however, creates additional problems. The first is that the detective's presence was apparently unknown to all of the members of the household: Hibbs exclaims (2.IV), "You were at Sir Roger's house!…and we weren't even aware of it! You must admit, that's very strange!" (It will be revealed later that Hibbs himself was in the same house at the time of the murder, and was likely in a position to know who was staying there.) Further, Burke says that "the killer was somebody well-known to the members of the household; the statements made by the servants were positive on that point, *that* [at the time of Sir Roger's murder] *nobody else had come into the house*" (2.IV). The latter statement would seem to confirm Hibbs' remark that no one in the household (other than Sir Roger himself) was aware of Burke's presence.

A second problem is that Burke states (2.IV), "I was in Sir Roger's house the night he was killed, but, as I was in my bedroom at the precise moment of his death, *I had no way of knowing how the murder had taken place.*" Apart from the fact that a bedroom (or "apartments" [1.III]) could not have been provided for him without the servants' knowledge – especially the butler's – Burke makes no claim that he heard the gunshot himself. He nonetheless (1.I) had expressed skepticism when the butler Williams claimed that he, Williams, did not hear the shot on the day Sir Roger was murdered – a skepticism that we subsequently find to be justified because Williams actually did hear it (2.IV); and it was also heard by Lucile and Hibbs upstairs, upon which "the sound of the gunfire had plunged the whole house into turmoil" and "Doors [were] being slammed" (2.IV).

Upon hearing the shot Williams went immediately to the crime scene, saw Sir James place the murder weapon in Sir Roger's hand, and then had time to bargain with Sir James about keeping silent – and then, further, Sir James had time enough to depart without being noticed by anyone even though the whole house was in "turmoil" – all of this happening before Burke, residing in the same house, showed up. To judge by his delay of several minutes in arriving at the crime scene, the detective seems to have been the *only* person who did *not* hear the shot. The novel, then, accurately includes (from the film) Hibbs' challenge to Burke on how the detective arrived so quickly, a significant problem that the film does not resolve. The novelist, however, in creating his own solution, did so at the price of creating the additional problem of why Burke was so *late* in arriving, given that he was already in the house and within hearing distance of the shot that everyone else heard.

This is by no means the only instance in which Mr. Boisyon's solution to a real problem in the film winds up generating additional problems within his own narrative.

Burke's changed appearance and his connection (or lack of connection) to Scotland Yard

Another of the problems with the film itself is that the Chaney character, Detective Burke, appears in the middle of the film in *two* makeups that are very different from how he appears, undisguised, at the beginning and end of the film. One is his guise as the vampire character; the other is as a different 'persona' of his same character as the detective. In the film, when Burke returns to the story five years after the initial murder of Sir Roger, he has been called in by Sir James this time to investigate the mysterious goings-on at the adjacent Balfour [**FrN**: Bradford] house, now apparently haunted. But at his reappearance he introduces himself with a business card (**CC**: "FADE IN Insert of card"), after which Sir James gives the butler directions, saying "*Professor* Burke is to be our house-guest, Williams. Have rooms prepared for him." In the film as released there are no explanations for why "Detective" Burke is now representing himself as "Professor" Burke, or for his significantly changed physical appearance: many surviving still photos show that his hair is much grayer; it is parted in the center rather than the side; he has long sideburns; he is dressed in a much lighter-shaded suit; he carries a cane; he habitually wears pince-nez glasses; and he is much more stiff-necked in posture.

What seems most plausible, if the alteration is to have any coherence with the rest of the story, is that this 'changed' Burke is deliberately distancing himself from his Scotland Yard affiliation, and that this distance from his former persona as an official detective is now being represented and reinforced visually – certainly a legitimate method for a silent film to convey important information. Repeatedly, when other characters insist on bringing in outside police to investigate the suspicious activities at the haunted Balfour house, Burke's response is emphatically to reject calls for any such involvement (**CC**: Burke: "I don't want the police in this!").

The origin of the problem of Burke's changes in both self-designation and physical appearance lies in what was 'lost on the cutting room floor'. In the original shooting script by Waldemar Young (not the final **CC** compiled by Reynolds and Browning) Burke was not present at all at the murder-scene of Sir Roger Balfour; none of the other characters laid eyes on him at that point; they don't meet him for the first time until five years later, and at that point none know that he is actually a Scotland Yard detective when he shows up. To summarize the rather unbelievable plot of the "The Hypnotist" script, Burke was aware from a distance that the death of Sir Roger was suspicious; and on the occasion of the more recent death of Sir Roger's son and heir – a plot line not in the released film – he decides to insinuate himself into Sir James's household in order to test his theory that hypnosis can be used to bring about a criminal's confession. He thus creates a different persona for himself, with a different physical appearance from his normal look – the latter identity is not revealed to any of the other characters until the end of the film – and he calls himself "Colonel Yates". In this guise he then passes himself off as "an old friend" of Sir James "from India" – an acquaintance whom Sir James does not remember (because no such person existed), but who nonetheless persuades Sir James of his *bona fides* simply through his commanding presence and hypnotic gaze. It is Burke as Col. Yates who emphatically rejects the calls for outside police involvement because he wants to keep Sir James completely under his own influence, with no outside referents who would diminish the detective's personal dominance. His aim to weaken Sir James' mental state in order to make him more susceptible to hypnotism, under which, Burke believes, he can be led to re-enact his crime in front of witnesses.

In other words, the film was shot with Chaney made up as Col. Yates, but the plot line with a second murder was eliminated at the cutting stage – quite possibly because that Yates deception was so unbelievable. The Chaney character then had to be introduced at the beginning of the film (at the scene of the sole murder, of Sir Roger) – and without the Yates makeup, as there would be no reason for Burke to assume such a disguise at that point, as he was simply functioning in his official capacity as a bona fide Scotland Yard detective. Sir James thus gets to know him at the very beginning of the film; and it is this prior acquaintance that motivates the baronet to call Burke "back in" five years later to investigate to suspicious activities at the haunted house adjacent to Sir James's own country estate. Even though Sir James was the murderer five years ago he has no reason to fear Burke, because he believes he successfully deceived the detective to conclude that the death of Sir Roger was a case of suicide.

In the released version of the film, *some* justification – minimal though it is – had to be provided for Burke's significantly changed appearance; and it plausibly lies in his new self-designation as "Professor" rather than "Detective", along with the alterations in physical appearance that visually distance him from his previous look *as* a Scotland Yard detective. This in turn provides some rationale for his adamant refusal to accede to both Sir James' and Hibbs' demands to "call the police": Burke won't do so because, in one sense, he still *is* "the police"; but in another he is now a "Professor" who is deliberately distancing himself from his police affiliation because wants no outside interference *from* the police, whose presence would undermine Burke's own careful manipulation of the baronet's mental state.

Apart from showing Burke's change in self-designation from "Detective" to "Professor", however, the film itself does nothing more to *explain why* Burke (in his new appearance) wants so vehemently to avoid calling in outside police. The reason lies in the fact that the original shooting script presents the detective's first appearance *as* Burke (rather than as Col. Yates) at a time subsequent to a second murder (that of Sir Roger's son); Burke first appears in the office of his Scotland Yard superior. There – before he has met any of the other characters in the story – he explains why he wants to put himself into Sir James' household: it is because he has always had suspicions about the original verdict of murder (even though he was not then involved in the case), *and* because he sees the present situation as giving him an opportunity to test his theory that hypnosis can be used to induce a criminal to re-enact his crime.

This script scene with Burke and his superior, however, was cut from the film as released; in the latter, it was unnecessary to have such a scene *introducing* Burke to the audience because, in the new plot line, he had *already* made himself known at the very beginning, at the scene of Sir Roger's death. A major problem for the resultant film, then, is that having cut the original scene (in the shooting script) of Detective Burke's introduction, it *also* thereby eliminated his explanation to his superior of why he wanted to get involved in the first place: to test his theory of hypnosis. The result is that the film's audience has no clue as to *why* the Chaney character acts as he does during most of the story; his behavior in vehemently rejecting all outside police interference seems unmotivated, although the action at the climax of the film – the re-enactment of the murder of Sir Roger – does indicate, *very* late in the game, that he intends to use hypnosis to bring it about. It is also a legitimate criticism of the film that its released version does not provide *sufficient* justification for his noticeable change in physical appearance from how he looked to all of the same characters five years previously. It is no wonder that many contemporary reviews of the film noted the incoherence of its story.

Mr. Boisyvon gets around one of the problems in the film – that of the Chaney character's radically different appearance as "Professor" – *by simply not mentioning that any such change has taken place.* In the novel, a visual alteration in Burke's appearance is not necessary as a means to emphasize his desire to distance himself from the formal connection to Scotland Yard that he had at the beginning of the story, five years earlier. In the novel, when Burke re-appears all those years after the murder of Sir Roger – having been called in by Sir James to investigate the nearby haunted house – he presents a calling card that reads:

> *Edward C. Burke*
> *Criminologist*
> *Saint-Charles Hotel.*
> *LONDON, S.W.*

Note that it does not say "Professor"; more important, however, at this point the novel also indicates more clearly than the "Professor" label alone (as in the **CC**) that the Chaney character is no longer claiming any connection to the agency. Indeed, after the presentation of this card the novel continues immediately with the following passage (1.III):

> Lucile looked up with astonishment.
> "Burke!" she exclaimed, "but isn't that the detective who made the official report of suicide five years ago?"
> Sir James nodded in confirmation.
> "It's one and the same," he said. "Given that it's proving impossible to find out anything, and in view of the surprising facts that I've since discovered, I determined to engage the services of a private detective. I remembered Burke, and went to see him this very afternoon..."

The narrative continues three paragraphs later:

> "What do you expect me to do? I just thought that Mr. Burke, who is familiar with our family tragedy, could be more useful to me than anyone else. Perhaps he didn't show great skill when the body [of Sir Roger] was discovered, I grant you that, but I can assure you nonetheless that he still remembers all the details, to this very

day. Would you believe, my visit didn't seem to cause him the slightest astonishment? You would almost have thought he was expecting me. And yet, he hasn't been a member of the official police force for the past two years."

Several other passages in the novel emphasize that Burke, now called back by Sir James, is not trying either to *hide* or to *minimize* his affiliation with Scotland Yard (as in the film); rather, he no longer has that formal connection at all. Indeed, he has been fired by Yard for his unconventional investigative methods:

> 1.III: [Sir James]: "he hasn't been a member of the official police force for the past two years"…"he now has much more freedom than in the past"

* * *

> 1.V: [Lucile]: "He was part of His Majesty's police for a long time."

> [Hibbs]: "But he's no longer part of the police force….I can tell you that Burked was *forced* to resign. It's said in the police stations that it was because of his unorthodox methods, which weren't at all in accordance with those permitted by law. They say he used to go too far when he was trying to extract confessions from suspects, but despite persistent enquiries I haven't been able to find out exactly what his methods consisted of. The one thing that's certain is that his resignation was forced upon him, and under threat of being struck off the official register of existing and former police officers."

* * *

> 2.I: [Hibbs]: "a man who was gotten rid of by Scotland Yard, as you were, for reasons that nobody wants to reveal, may very well be a dishonest man"…

[Burke]: "you've made reference to my resignation from Scotland Yard, and you've cast doubt on my integrity. I don't need to justify myself to you, of course; however, I imagine you'd like to know why I left the official police force."... "Quite simply because I believe in hypnotism.... It is thanks to the power of hypnosis that I have obtained my greatest successes in criminal investigation, but I must admit that this method isn't part of the usual procedures of our British police force. The individual liberty of human beings is sacrosanct, as you know, and every criminal has the right not to say anything, if he doesn't think it's useful to his defense. To extract from him, by a scientific method, the decisive admission of guilt that his conscience forbids him to make is not considered compelling evidence. But, my dear Sir, I swear to you that I've never used this method, save in exceptional cases and always in a perfectly controlled manner."

*   *   *

2.V: "Mr. Burke," the Chief Magistrate continued, "you have investigated the Sir Roger Bradford murder case outside the aegis of the official police force; and in doing so, you've made use of certain methods for which you've already been severely reprimanded."...

The Chief Magistrate was listening to the detective with visible interest, and he was beginning to regret that the police force was now deprived of the services of a man of such high competence. There could no longer be any question of reprimanding or admonishing him.

In sum, the French novel thus departs from the cutting continuity in presenting Burke not as hiding or minimizing his continued Scotland Yard affiliation, but as having lost it entirely.

Nevertheless, the novelist has re-introduced Burke's motivation – his interest in hypnotism, even if the implications of it are not yet clear to the other characters – and has done it at a point in the story prior to the detective's actual use of that method of crime-solving. The writer thus improves the coherence of the story by laying a groundwork for its climax in a way that the film itself does not.

The question arises, then, how does Burke enforce his authority over Sir James and Hibbs when both demand that he call in outside police, especially since both are aware that he is no longer with Scotland Yard? The novelist provides this rationale:

> 1.IV: [Burke to Sir James]: "But Burke replied categorically, and with a sort of repressed rage: 'I don't need the police! We will deal with this case ourselves, and if you instruct anyone outside of this house to conduct a search, I will immediately withdraw my services.'
>
> "His tone of voice, which brooked no disagreement, had the desired impact on the master of the house, who didn't say anything further."

In 1.VII Burke again successfully asserts his personal – not institutional – authority.

The several photos of Chaney-as-Burke included in this photoplay edition novel do indeed convey the impression of a forceful, dominating, and even overbearing character; so his physical appearance does indeed help to emphasize the force behind the words by which he emphasizes his personal authority (both in the novel and in the film itself). However, the last photo of Burke included in the French novel shows Chaney without his "carry-over" Col. Yates makeup – the stiff-necked appearance he took on to aid in dominating Sir James' household in the absence of all Scotland Yard affiliation. According to other surviving sources for the film, including still photos, this very different dark-haired look of Burke, with no sideburns, is just how he appeared in the film at the beginning of the story, in the scene of his appearance at Sir Roger's murder. While the French novel may be internally consistent in not mentioning the change in the detective's appearance, it thereby leaves unexplained an inconsistency in the photos with which it is illustrated: its last photo of Burke-as-detective, at the end of the story, shows him holding the hand of Lucile (actress Marceline Day) while Hibbs (Conrad Nagel) looks on; and Burke, here, has dark hair, dark trousers, no pince-nez glasses, and no sideburns.

Yet another problem with the novel is that Burke, while clearly *not* having a formal affiliation with Scotland Yard – he had been fired – nevertheless *acts* as though he does indeed maintain that official authority. He is clearly supervising the servant Betty, who all along has been an undercover agent working for him:

2.II: [Burke]: "This is good work, Betty. You are an assistant worthy of promotion, and my report to Inspector Bryce will be completely favorable to you"...[Betty]: "Thank you, Mr. Burke; a reference from you will, moreover, be very useful to me, because I've applied to become part of the counter-espionage brigade."

* * *

2.V: [Burke to Hibbs]: "Betty, the very worthy assistant whom I trained myself, played the part of a terrified servant to perfection."

Further, Burke is clearly supervising Inspector Bryce, too, who does most of the masquerading as the vampiric "professor" and who unmistakably *is* a Scotland Yard agent. Betty's Scotland Yard status as a policewoman is also evident in that she has the power of arrest (2.III: [Burke]: "Arrest him, Miss Adams! And advise him that anything he says from this moment onwards may be used against him in a court of law"). And Burke shows that he himself retains the same power of arrest (2.IV: [Burke]: "But I'm arresting you in the name of His Majesty the King"), which he would not have any claim to after his dismissal. The fact that he was still in that "fired" status at the time of the arrests is made clear in his subsequent interview with the Yard's Chief Magistrate (2.V: "Mr. Burke," the Chief Magistrate continued, "you have investigated the Sir Roger Bradford murder outside the aegis of the official police force"). These inconsistencies in the novel are simply left unresolved.

The length of the maid/cook's employment

Another anomaly in the novel concerns the length of Betty's employment in Sir James' household:

1.IV: [Hibbs]: "It was *Betty, the cook*, who tipped me off about the existence of this book, and she herself showed me the place where it was kept in the library."

1.IV: [Sir James]: "*The cook* has only been in my employment *for two years*."

In the film (**CC**), where this character is called Smithson rather than Betty, and she is a maid rather than a cook, it is made clear that she is "the *new* maid"; and at one point she addresses the gardener saying, "I'm a lucky prune…. *workin' a fortnight* already in the same 'house'old with a handsome gent like you."

In the film, then, this character has been in Sir James' household for two weeks; in the novel, for two years. This raises additional unanswered questions in the novel concerning how Burke – who was fired two years ago by Scotland Yard – came to be her supervisor at all in her role as an undercover agent *for* the Yard. The novelist, apparently realizing the problem, provides a rather lame, tacked-on explanation at the end of the story, simply with a wave of his authorial hand:

> 2.V: [re: Harris]: "At first, the Welshman hadn't wanted to believe that Betty had played so important a role in Sir James' house. When he realized that she had really belonged to such a respectable British institution as the official Police force, he remained speechless for at least half a day…*Betty had only joined the police force after this investigation, but she was already in a position to exercise some influence there.*"

Evidently readers are to believe that a woman working as a cook for two years was only recently recruited by Burke as a confederate – not implausible by itself – but that within that short time period she also became a full-fledged member of the police force, with the power of arrest – also advancing to "a position to exercise some power" at Scotland Yard – without any outside training-time or absence from Sir James' household that would have noticeably interfered with her full-time cook's job there. And, further, she received that training from someone who had himself been fired from the Yard because of his unacceptable investigative methods.

Finding the suicide note

At another point in the novel its author solves a different problem that stands out prominently in the film, but again he does it in a way that creates additional unanswered questions in his own story.

In the film, Sir James shows Burke the original 'suicide' note written by Sir Roger just before he was murdered, as a handwriting sample to compare to the signature on the new lease signed by the vampire character for the mansion next door. Burke reacts with feigned surprise at seeing it; supposedly it had been locked away in Burke's possession back at Scotland Yard:

> **CC:** [Burke]""Sir James, how did they ever get this out of my desk?"

In the film, no explanation is given for its re-appearance in Sir James' desk.

In the novel, however, Burke elaborates:

> 1.III: [Burke]: "How on earth did anybody manage to get hold of this note? It was locked away in my records, in the middle of the case file, and it's clearly the same document. Look, in the corner, you can still see the number 'eight' that indicates its file reference. That figure was written by me in pencil on the note, five years ago. I recognize it only too well."

The same 1.III sequence indicates that the signature on the note is believed to be in the same handwriting as that on the lease. It is evident – although not to Sir James, nor to the audiences of the film or the novel – that the note must have been given by Burke to Smithson/Betty, his confederate in the household, to plant where the baronet would find it. In the film, however, this is never explained; and in the novel Burke's frank admission that the note somehow ("How on earth") was taken from his Scotland Yard files is itself problematic, because the alleged theft would have taken place at a time when he would not have had access to those files himself, having been fired two years previously.

Sir Roger's tomb

The novelist makes a minor change from the film in another area. In both sources, Sir James and Burke have seen what is apparently the dead Sir Roger's signature on the new lease to the "haunted" house next door;

but in order to verify that he is indeed dead they make a nocturnal foray to inspect his tomb. In the film, Sir James sees for himself that it is empty:

> **CC:** [Sir James to Burke]: "Burke! The tomb is empty! Balfour is gone!"

> **CC:** [Sir James, later]: "But Burke…you've got to admit that Balfour's tomb was empty!"

In the novel (1.III), however, only Burke actually looks into the tomb. We then find only later what really happened when Burke explains:

> 2.V: "I simply confined myself to lightly lifting the lid of the coffin, and I was the only one to look into it that night because Sir James, in a state of extreme distress, remained standing at the door of the tomb."

The presence of outside detectives

In the film, in spite of Burke's repeated rejection of calls for outside detectives to be at hand, at least four nevertheless show up at the climax of the film – having evidently been called in secretly to make sure that his plan to trap Sir James runs smoothly. Two of them escort Sir James from his own house into the grounds of the neighboring mansion. At the same time that this is taking place two others, already in the haunted mansion, are physically subduing Hibbs who has climbed into the house through a window in a heroic attempt to rescue Lucille, whom he believes to have been abducted by the vampire and his cohorts. Immediately after Hibbs' capture, Burke – who has apparently run across the grounds before Sir James and his detective escorts have had time to arrive – "enters with costume" (**CC**) and instructs another confederate to continue making himself up as the deceased Sir Roger, while he (Burke) goes out in that costume of the "old man" who is "grinning hideously" – i.e., as the vampire character – to meet Sir James. At this point the two detectives escorting Sir James have receded, "hiding behind trees"; and Burke now successfully hypnotizes the terrified Sir James, telling him twice, "It is five years ago…you are at Roger Balfour's house."

Sir James is then admitted to the haunted mansion by the butler, who, in the film, is now working for Burke in voluntarily recreating his own innocent actions as he performed them that same "five years ago" in order to facilitate, according to Burke's plan, the baronet's recreation of his own guilty action. (In the French novel this butler shares in the guilt of concealing Sir James as the murder; in the film he has no such secret to hide.)

When Sir James does indeed re-enact his murder of Sir Roger, he is then seized and held by two detectives who with Burke have witnessed the action. Burke, at this point, is still in his vampire makeup; he is described in the cutting continuity shortly afterward: "MLS [medium long shot] dressing room showing Burke wiping make up from face. Lucille enters and begins to thank him as Burke takes hold of her hands."

The French novel changes several aspects of this scenario: it eliminates the extra detectives entirely until after Sir James and the butler Williams have been arrested; Burke then says (FrN2.III): "Betty, I'm going to ask you to be kind enough to call the three inspectors *who are in the garden* so that they can take care of our prisoners."

Other variant details of the re-enactment of the crime

- In the novel, Burke, *not* disguised as the vampire, has already hypnotized Sir James prior to the latter's walk, unaccompanied by any detectives, to the haunted mansion.

- In the novel, Burke has also hypnotized Hibbs to put him, too, in the mindset that he will act just as he did five years ago. This puts him peacefully in Lucile's company within the same house in which the murder takes place; but, in spite of his hearing a gunshot and the ensuing commotion, he does not realize that any crime has been committed, so he simply walks back to Sir James' mansion, where he is told a few minutes later by the baronet that Sir Roger is dead. In the film, he had previously been hypnotized in his room by Burke, who apparently (with no indication to the audience) concluded at that point that Hibbs was not the murderer.

    Subsequently, Lucille is supposedly sealed in her room with various tokens to ward off vampires; but when Burke, Hibbs, and Sir James knock on her door, and then break in to find her absent and the room in shambles, Hibbs is un-hypnotized at this point (in the **CC**) and under the belief that Lucille is in danger; hence his attempt to save her. In the film, Lucille's disappearance had been pre-arranged by Burke with her consent – although the audience is given no clear indication that this is the situation – to get her into the other house, so that she will there enact her own part in the recreation of the crime. The un-hypnotized Hibbs' forceful detention by the two detectives at the other house, then, is done to prevent him from ruining the operation of Burke's plan for that re-enactment. Lucille's mysterious disappearance, which has the unanticipated byproduct of Hibbs' attempt to rescue her, is supposedly – i.e, not clearly – staged to begin with in order intentionally to further agitate Sir James, to make him mentally more susceptible to the hypnotic state in which he will very soon be placed.

- In the novel, Burke *also* hypnotizes Lucile, to put her into the "five years ago" state. In the film she simply voluntarily re-enacts what she did at that time, trusting in what Burke had told her, that doing so would contribute to the discovery of her father's murderer.

- In the novel, it is Inspector Bryce, not the butler, who admits Sir James into Sir Roger's house. And, somewhat illogically for the plot, Sir James in his hypnotized state does not recognize that this is not the person who was at the door five years ago.

- In the novel, the butler Williams was complicit in concealing Sir James' crime, partly to prevent a scandal that would destroy the reputation of the family he has served for so long, and partly for the money that Sir James offers him. In the film, however, he is completely innocent and does not see Sir James at the murder scene – minutes before, however, he does re-enact his own role in admitting Sir James into the murder house, and he does it voluntarily in cooperation with Burke's plan to bring the murderer to justice.

- In the novel, Williams in company with Burke witnesses Sir James placing the gun in the hands of the 'deceased' actor playing the role of Sir Roger. But when Williams then refuses to re-enact his own dialogue with the murderer, Burke himself, "turning toward the killer" (2.III), directly addresses Sir James with the words he infers that Williams would have said. Since Burke is still in his vampire guise at this point (discussed below), once again the novel's plot illogically requires Sir James not to realize that the presence of this bizarre creature does not at all fit into the murder-scene activity as it transpired "five years ago." In the film, while Sir James had indeed been hypnotized by Burke in his vampire makeup, he (Sir James) does not see him again until Burke (still in vampire mode) snaps him *out* of his mesmerized condition, *after* he has re-enacted the murder before multiple witnesses.

- In the **CC**, Burke and two detectives witness the murder re-enactment. In the novel, Burke alone sees the re-enacted crime, although the butler Williams is then summoned in time to witness, with Burke, Sir James' placement of the gun into the 'deceased' Sir Roger's hand. The fact that *only* Burke – and the soon-to-be-dead Sir James – hears Williams' confession that he did indeed cover up the crime (to protect the family) is referred to later, as a reason to dismiss any charges against Williams (2.V). (The presence of the actor who is still portraying the 'dead' Sir Roger is not referred to in the novel; apparently we must believe he did not hear the conversation between the detective and the butler.) In any event, in the novel's plot the glaring lack of the simple expedient of having multiple witnesses (beyond Burke himself and the 'dead' actor) to the re-enacted murder seriously undermines what, up to then, has been a very detailed plan to bring the murderer to justice. The novelist does assert, however, that "The detective then turned to the people who had witnessed this scene" [2.IV] – but the scene referred to was not the murder itself, nor Williams' confession, but rather only the confession of Sir James. Had they heard Williams' confession as well, the subsequent justification for not prosecuting him would not hold up – i.e., Burke's statement to his Scotland Yard superior [2.V]:

> "I think," he went on, speaking more and more slowly, as though carefully weighing his words, "that we should have the case against Williams dismissed, because, in actual fact, I'm the only one who knows about his confession."

- Immediately prior to the assemblage of the cast of characters at the murder re-enactment scene, the film does create the impression that Lucille had been abducted from her bedroom by the vampire – which is what sets Hibbs off on his aborted rescue mission. In the novel, Burke has Lucile hide herself in a curtained balcony above the dining room, before her bedroom is sealed against intruders, there to await the cook Betty who then escorts her into the other house. It is while this is going on that Burke, undisguised, hypnotizes Hibbs; and Hibbs then recreates his own action of "five years ago" in joining Lucile in Sir Rogers' house, there asserting his love for her. Indeed, by this time Burke has *also* hypnotized Lucile, to put her into the same "five years ago" time frame. (In the film, it is *only* Sir James who is hypnotized for the re-enactment drama.) The novel thus entirely eliminates both Hibbs' belief (in the **CC**) that Lucile is in danger and his dramatic attempt to rescue her, with its possibility that he might spoil Burke's overall scheme at the last minute. The novel has Burke hypnotizing Sir James *and* Hibbs *and* Lucile.

- The novel does solve some other confusing problems in the film, the first concerning how Lucille has been conducted from her house to the haunted mansion. When (in the **CC**) Burke, Hibbs, and Sir James break into her wreath-and-sword-protected room in Sir James' house to find she is gone – apparently abducted by the vampire – it is indicated by an intertitle that the maid Smithson has also disappeared. Her next appearance is at Burke's side, both hidden from the sight of Sir James, at the start of the crime's re-enactment. Her appearance then and there thus indicates that somehow she did indeed come next door to the haunted house – although there is no explicit mention of her having escorted Lucille – *and* it reveals *now* that she is a confederate of the detective in carrying out his scheme. This, in turn, gives the audience a new take on earlier sequences in the film. It becomes evident at this point that the elaborate account she had previously given of being chased by the vampire inside Sir James' own house (filmed as a dreamlike "DISSOLVE" sequence to show what she claimed to have experienced) *must* have been entirely fictional, concocted according to Burke's plan of scaring Sir James. It also becomes clear in retrospect that her having been employed by Sir James for a mere two weeks – i.e., *not* having been a long-time family retainer – is also significant.

In the novel, however, Burke mentions explicitly that Lucile has been conducted next door by "our loyal Betty" (2.II); and the fact that she's been working as an undercover policewoman for Burke is subsequently elaborated in many details not mentioned at all in the film.

- Another situation that is confusing in the film is clarified in the novel. This has to do with the way that the film shows Lucille's treatment upon her arrival at the murder house to play her part in the reconstruction of the crime. In the cutting continuity she has, in a previous scene, acknowledged her trust in Burke:

> [Burke]: "I am going to ask you to put yourself in my hands....to do whatever I say....no matter how trying it may be."
> [Lucille]: "Mr. Burke, you make me feel that I should trust you....that you are my friend."

And shortly afterward:

> [Burke to Lucille]: "Be brave, my dear. Follow my instructions tonight."

It will become apparent only subsequently what those instructions were, that Burke has asked her to play the part, unhypnotized, of herself five years ago at the murder scene, in acting as the young daughter of "the stranger" – the designation given in the **CC** to Burke's confederate – who will be impersonating her dead father. In the film, however, when she arrives at the haunted mansion she encounters both "the stranger" – here, made up as the vampire character just before turning over that costume to Burke, who has not yet arrived – and the "Bat girl" Luna; and rather confusingly, both remain "in character" in ways that frighten Lucille, even though both know that she has been let in on the plot and that, indeed, she has her own part to play. Indeed, Lucille regards Luna "with [an] expression of horror" and "tries to get away from her" when she "bares Lucille's shoulder" in attempting to get Lucille to change into a different dress, to make her look as she appeared in five years ago. Further, Lucille's genuine fright at the appearance of the vampire (i.e., "the stranger", not Burke) and Luna is not lessened by the presence of her friend the butler, who in the film continuity is also now about to play his part too, unhypnotized, in admitting Sir James at the front door. None of the characters, then, seeks to assuage her fear; and the film leaves the visual impression that she is indeed in peril in the haunted house; this is confirmed by several still photos. (A problem for the film narrative, then, is that only moments later she is agreeably and smilingly playing her necessary part in the crime reconstruction.)

In the novel (2.III), we read that "Lucile, just as she had promised Mr. Burke, followed Betty without hesitation and without displaying the slightest fear." Her subsequent momentary fright at seeing Burke – who has indeed already arrived – in the vampire guise is immediately laid to rest when Burke "hastened to remove his false teeth and mask." One of the still photos accompanying the novel, however, shows both the vampire (Chaney) and the Bat girl both doing their best to scare the young woman; and so a problem that Mr. Boisyvan largely solves in his narrative is undercut by his (or perhaps an editor's?) choice of this illustration to accompany the text.

- A further confusion in the film itself is that Burke's confederate who is referred to as "the stranger" is indeed *in the vampire makeup and costume*, which he is about to switch with Burke so that the latter can then go out to meet the approaching Sir James and hypnotize him into thinking it is "five years ago." The same character, designated by the same "the stranger" appellation in the continuity, then goes on to change his own makeup *into that of the fake Sir Roger*, to play that part in the murder re-enactment while Burke then continues as the vampire. The problem is that earlier in the film in the **CC** sequence in which both Burke and Sir James spied into the haunted mansion, they saw "Roger Balfour & 2 men in room, bat girl in b.g. [background] starts to fly toward f.g. [foreground']," at which point Sir James exclaims "Burke…. look! It <u>is</u> Roger Balfour!" The **CC** in this earlier scene offers additional information that contradicts its later narrative (and also diverges from the French novel):

> LS [long shot] *Man with high hat & cloak with back to camera.* Another man sitting beside him, and *Roger Balfour sitting in chair in front of them.* MCU [medium close up] *Andy* at window looking off scene.
> MS Burke & Sir James, start to climb up ladder.

Clearly, the "Man in the high hat" [the vampire] and Sir Roger are not portrayed by the same person. We find out only at the very end of the **CC** that this "Andy" is the theatrical partner of the Bat girl. In the French novel, however, it is this "music-hall performer" – not specifically named – and *not* "the stranger" of the **CC** who has been hired to impersonate the deceased Sir Roger. As Burke says in the novel (2.V):

> "It was then that I set about 'resurrecting' Sir Roger. It took me a certain amount of time to find an actor who could play that part. But I found him in the person of an excellent music-hall performer, accustomed to acting and to wearing disguises and costumes, a performer who, with his variety-show partner Luna, became my associate over the course of a few days."

The whole skein is rather complicated at this point because it involves three elements: not just the **CC** and the **FrN** but the **still photo** showing Sir Roger and the back of the vampire character. Among the inconsistencies:

1. In the **CC** we have the Sir Roger impersonator and the vampire facing each other, a situation that is contradicted elsewhere in the **CC** in that it shows that the two are both played sequentially by one and the same person ("the stranger") just before the re-enactment scene. We also have "2 men" in addition, one of whom is "sitting beside" the vampire character but neither of whom is identified. We additionally have "Andy" apparently serving as a lookout for the group to alert them to the approach of Burke and Sir James. We do not find out until the very

end of the film, however, that he is the bat girl's theatrical partner. *His* appearance here, however, does tie in to the **CC**'s final exposition that the whole haunted house staging was a ruse. The **CC**, further, has it that "bat girl in b.g. [background] starts to fly toward f.g. [foreground]" – not the novel's unidentified "ectoplasm".

2. In the **FrN** we have in this scene only Sir Roger (played by the "variety show" performer hired by Burke), the vampire (played by Bryce), and Luna; there is no "lookout" nor are there any extra "2 men". However, in the novel it is not Luna who is witnessed as eerily "flying" but rather a separate, mysterious "floating ectoplasm" that is never explained.

3. The **still photo** shows only three characters as those (apparently) who come to be witnessed by Burke and Sir James: The Sir Roger impersonator, the vampire (seen only from behind), and a third man "sitting beside" him (in agreement with the **CC**) who remains mysteriously unidentified; there is no Bat girl present. It is evident from other surviving still photos (included in the **FrN**) that the actor seen here impersonating Sir Roger is the same one who impersonates him during the later re-enactment of the crime. (He is identified in the **CC**'s opening credits, in a FADE IN shot to the CAST list, as "The Stranger.... Claude King.") The inconsistency here is, again, that the same **CC** (after this "spying" scene) has this actor playing both the vampire and Sir Roger – it is he who switches from one makeup to the other, handing off the vampire disguise to Burke – just before the re-enactment scene; but in the photo the 'dead' baronet and the vampire are obviously not played simultaneously by the same actor. What the photo depicts is thus inconsistent with the **CC** in this regard, and also with the **FrN** in showing a third, unidentified man sitting next to the vampire character. Its omission of Luna is not necessarily problematic in regard to either the **CC** or the **FrN**.

One gun or two guns at the re-enactment

The cutting continuity indicates that during the scene in which the hypnotized Sir James re-enacts his crime, he initially approaches the fake Sir Roger (a Burke confederate referred to as the "stranger", made up to look like the victim) with one gun, which Sir James has brought to the scene himself:

> **CC:** "Sir James comes in from b.g. [background] with gun in hand and confronts stranger."

An immediate problem within the film is that the continuity does not explain how this weapon came into Sir James's possession to begin with; he must have had it on him already when, moments before, he met Burke outside in his vampire guise and became hypnotized by him. (There is no indication that Burke gave him the gun at that time.) Further, the **CC** provides no indication that this gun, which the hypnotized baronet intends to use in shooting the fake Sir Roger, is loaded with blanks instead of real bullets to prevent the death of the impersonator.

Minutes later, after Sir James and the fake Sir Roger have argued over the future of Lucille, Sir James leaves but then surreptitiously returns; the cutting continuity reads:

> MS [medium shot] stranger in chair behind desk. Sir James with gun in hand in partition in b.g. [background]
>
> MCU [medium close up] Burke hiding by corner of room.
>
> MLS [medium long shot] room showing stranger in chair behind desk. Sir James come in from b.g. with gun in hand and confronts the stranger.

Sir James then instructs the fake Sir Roger – "the stranger" – to write out a suicide note:

> "Take paper…and write what I tell you!"
>
> MS Sir James confronting stranger threateningly and finishing title and reaching into drawer for gun.

CU [close up] of hand grabbing hand holding gun.

MS Sir James confronting stranger, reaching into drawer
for gun.

What has just happened is that the fake Sir Roger has attempted to pull a
gun of out of his own desk drawer, and Sir James has wrested the weapon
away from him. Sir James then repeats his demand that "the stranger"
write out a dictated suicide note, followed by:

MS stranger writing, Sir James aiming both guns at him.

CU Burke listening

MS At Sir James' back as he confronts stranger. Smoke is
seen of a shot fired. Sir James puts his right hand gun into
pocket. Stranger slumps forward and down on floor....

A surviving still photo does indeed show Sir James (actor Henry Walthall)
holding two guns on the impersonator of Sir Roger. The problem is that
no indication has been given in the **CC** that *either* gun has been loaded in
advance with blanks. And yet, of course, the impersonator is not killed
by the "shot fired."

This glaring problem in the **CC** is somewhat remedied in the French
novel. The argument between Sir James and the Roger impersonator ("the
actor") unfolds as follows (2.III); mention of a "banished" character refers
to an earlier suitor for Lucile. Note that Sir James' hands are initially empty:

"Yes," Sir James went on, "I know, you banished him from
your house...What? You will banish me too, if I insist...
no, you won't do that..."

He was panting, his hands were moving feverishly
and he was banging on the desk with his fist....

Sir James approached the actor as if he was going to
grab him by the shoulders; but he checked himself; his
arms were back at his side once more, and there was now
a look of panic in his eyes.

"No," he stammered, "no...you shall not treat me so
cruelly, you shall not banish me from this house. I'm not

a thief, as you are well aware, and I want Lucile for I love her with all my heart and soul; she's not going to become any other man's wife, I'll see to that – even if I have to..."

He stopped abruptly; his face lit up with an evil smile and chuckling, and, with frantic, impulsive speed, he opened the desk drawer, the small drawer on the right that was there directly in front of him since he was standing beside Sir Roger; and, thrusting his hand inside, he took a revolver out from it and, immediately, held the barrel of the gun against the actor's temple.

Although no explanation is given, it is implied that Sir James must have known, simply from their long acquaintance, that Sir Roger kept a gun in his desk. The novel's narrative continues:

The latter – despite being well-prepared for the inevitable conclusion of this dramatic scene – now looked, with a desperate appeal in his eyes, towards the corner where Burke stood concealed from view by the double curtains.

Unquestionably there was no bullet in that weapon kept in Sir Roger's desk drawer, but even if there was only powder in the chamber, its lethal effect would be practically the same, and the actor would certainly be killed by the discharge.

But, from behind the curtains, the detective made a sign to reassure him.

Burke listened attentively to every single word uttered by Sir James, not missing anything. The latter was now holding the barrel of the revolver against his cousin's forehead....

A moment later, after the actor has penned the dictated suicide note:

And, almost immediately, he pulled the trigger; there was only a muffled sound [*un brut sec*], but, at the same time, a bang reverberated.

It was the detective, who had emptied a bullet from his own revolver into the floor.

Since, we are told, there was unquestionably [*sans doute*] no bullet in the gun found in the drawer, it must be inferred that Burke has prepared the weapon beforehand; but, strangely, the fake Sir Roger at whom the gun is being pointed now looks toward him with a desperate appeal [*un regard déspéré*]. That the doctored gun does not contain either a real bullet or even enough powder with sufficient explosive force to cause harm seems to be a detail that was not conveyed to the actor in the hot seat. Once again, the French author has noticed a problem in the film (in which no indication of any prior doctoring of *either* gun is offered) and "solved" it rather carelessly: he prudently simplifies the situation by eliminating one gun entirely, but rather gingerly accounts for the remaining danger by another wave of his authorial hand only at the moment the problem becomes evident, without having laid any prior groundwork for either the gun's presence in the drawer (without which Sir James would have no murder weapon at all), its doctored state, or the actor's awareness of what is a crucial condition of the planned re-enactment.

Burke in the makeup of the vampire character

In the film itself there is no doubt the Lon Chaney himself appears in most of the scenes in which the vampire character is onscreen. The cutting continuity clearly indicates this in his first appearance, when he is observed by the maid Smithson and the gardener: [CC]: "Balfour Hall, *Burke & Bat Girl* coming downstairs." This is followed immediately by his meeting with the property's lease agents: "*Chaney* comes down to men at tree."

In the maid Smithson's "DISSOLVE" scene showing her made-up account of seeing the vampire inside Sir James's own house, however, the CC consistently refers to the character who appears here as "the vampire" and not as "Chaney" or "Burke." Nevertheless, the many surviving still photos of this scene clearly show that it is Chaney himself in the makeup during this episode. Immediately after the maid's account, however, she and the entire group to whom she has recounted her tale – Sir James, Lucille, Hibbs, and Burke – look out the window, to see (in the CC's words) "Vampire walks in garden." Clearly, this must be Burke's confederate down below, seen by the whole group only from a distance.

A subsequent sequence in the CC is confusing, however. It occurs immediately after Lucille tells the group in Sir James' house that she has heard the voice of her dead father "calling to me from the garden":

CU [close up] of Henry Walthall.

"Did you hear what she said….her father's voice!"

CU of Henry Walthall.

CU of Chaney.

CU of Henry Walthall.

"I shall never be satisfied until I see that Balfour
is in his tomb!"

LS [long shot] of Walthall and Chaney

FADE OUT

FADE IN
LS of cemetery. At tomb.

CU of owl in tree.

MS [medium shot] of 2 men with lantern.

"Burke! The tomb is empty! Balfour is gone!"

MS of man with lantern. They exit

LS of hall. Chaney, the bat girl and 2 men

FADE OUT

END OF REEL TWO

Evidently the immediate change of scene from the graveyard to the haunted mansion is meant to suggest visually to the audience that the reason Balfour's tomb is empty is that his missing body now really *is* alive again and in the presence of the vampire…except that, with no indication of any temporal change in the time sequence, Burke thus appears to be in two places simultaneously, both as Burke exiting from the cemetery and as the vampire (designated specifically as "Chaney" in the **CC**) in the haunted house. It is not Burke's confederate who appears as the vampire in this scene, as he does in the subsequent sequence in which both "Sir James & Burke" spy into the Balfour house and observe:

> LS room. Man with high hat & cloak with back to camera.
> Another man sitting beside him, and Roger Balfour
> sitting in the chair in front of them.

Here, it is obviously Burke's assistant who is dressed as the vampire because Chaney-as-Burke is observing him in company with Sir James, and we as audience cannot see the face of the man "with high hat & cloak."

The next appearance of the vampire character in the **CC** also has him played by "the stranger" – not Chaney – when he appears with the Luna and the butler at the point when Lucille has been brought over to the haunted house to prepare for playing her own part in the crime re-enactment. At this point the continuity reads:

> CU stranger & Bat girl. Stranger turns to Lucille and speaks.
> "Remember....Lucille....
> you....are....doing....
> this....for....your....
> father."

As mentioned before, both the "stranger" and the Bat girl both rather imprudently stay "in character" here in Lucille's presence, badly frightening her – as indicated by surviving still photos – even as they endeavor to lead her on to play her part.

Immediately following this **CC** sequence, Burke – still in Sir James' house – instructs the baronet to walk over to the house next door and to stare directly into the eyes of "Whomever you meet." This personage will be Burke himself, who quickly exits and goes to the haunted house, just in time to prevent Hibbs – who is not in on the planned re-enactment – from ruining the plan by breaking in through a window in an attempt to rescue Lucille, whom he believes to be in genuine danger. Once Hibbs is taken out of the way, the continuity continues:

> LS thru hallway-Burk closes door-double hands Burke
> custome [misspelling of *costume*] & exits-Burke exits in
> another direction.

> MS stranger making up as Burke enters with costume &
> speaks:
>
> "We're going to finish this tonight! Hurry up…
> make up like Balfour again!"

The "double" here is the same person as "the stranger" who has just instructed Lucille to play her part in the scheme. He has now transferred the vampire costume to Burke, his superior, and Burke now goes out in vampire guise to meet and hypnotize the approaching Sir James. In this sequence the **CC** refers to Burke, in makeup and costume, as the "old man" until after the hypnotism, when one of the concealed detectives "enters to him [i.e., to the "old man"]-Burke gives him instructions." The skeletal outline of the **CC** leaves no doubt that it is now Chaney-as-Burke who is in the "old man"/vampire makeup. Indeed, there is no indication that he abandons this appearance during the whole subsequent re-enactment of the crime, which "Burke" now observes from a concealed vantage. It is only *after* Sir James has been arrested and the crime has been solved that we find him *removing* his makeup:

> MLS [medium long shot] dressing room showing Burke
> wiping his make up from face. Lucille enters and begins to
> thank him…

(It is noteworthy that in the shooting script of "The Hypnotist" [reproduced in the Riley volumes] from which the cutting continuity is edited down, it is very clear that Burke is indeed still in his vampire makeup at the time of Sir James' arrest.)

In contrast to the film, a major peculiarity of the French novel is that at no point does it require us to imaginatively envision Lon Chaney as the Burke character in any makeup other than his "straight" appearance as the detective until one very brief stint as the vampire near the end of the book. Throughout most of the story it is Burke's assistant Inspector Bryce – not Burke himself – who enacts the role of the vampire, from his very first "appearances" as recounted to Sir James first by the maid Betty and Harris the gardener (1.II), and then immediately afterward by the baronet's solicitor, who has just confirmed the leasing of the next-door house to two very strange individuals.

The night-time sighting by Betty and Harris of the two does not give any details of the mysterious strangers' appearance other than that they "looked like two shadows"; but the two witnesses say insist they saw these strangers "nor more than ten minutes ago" – at a time when Burke and Sir James were together in the latter's house. Whoever the strange characters were, then, neither could be pictured by the French novel's readers as Burke in disguise.

Moments later, after Betty and Harris have left, Sir James receives a telephone call from his solicitor (1.III); the novel relates it as follows:

The story of the lease, as recounted by the solicitor, sent shivers down the spine of all who heard it.

He had recently received, in his office, a man who claimed to be a professor, but who didn't specify exactly what subjects he lectured in, and who was accompanied by a young woman who was, admittedly, exceedingly beautiful, but whose beauty was unusual, so out of the ordinary that the solicitor was quite at a loss to find words that would have been adequate to describe it.

"She was like a dead woman who had just recently emerged from her tomb..."

And he lowered his voice to a mere whisper, as though he were fearful of suddenly seeing the spectral apparition of that woman appear before his eyes.

The professor (we are still referring to the solicitor's description of him) was a man of about sixty, hunchbacked, stooped, and dressed in a dark Inverness cape to which he seemed to be surgically attached, so perpetually did he wear it, not even taking it off in the office.

"The thing that struck me most forcibly," said the solicitor, "was his strange, silent, sarcastic little laugh. It gave me the impression that this professor found it impossible to ever close his mouth. From his gums, constantly exposed to view, emerged two rows of sparkling teeth that gave his face a ferocious expression. One's eyes were constantly drawn to this bizarre set of teeth. They reminded me of those of some carnivorous beast, always at the ready to cruelly devour its prey."

When Sir James tries to meet the new tenant directly to complete the legal formalities with a signature, the latter "had not turned up at the first appointment that had been arranged." "[O]n the second day," however, the solicitor does acquire the new tenant's signature and immediately delivers it to the baronet: and it is the signature not of "the professor," but of the deceased Roger Bradford. It is clear that Burke did not want Sir James to see the fake actor portraying Sir Roger, and it is implied that "the professor" was not necessarily present at this signing meeting.

As with many other sequences in the novel that strain the reader's credibility, Burke's explanation of the need for a vampire character's presence at all is given by him in the last chapter (2.V):

> "It was obvious that the murderer would not confess to his crime unless he were forced to do so, and somehow subdued, as it were. But how could those ends be achieved? What needed to be done? In a nutshell, he would have to be put in a state of mind in which he would be absolutely incapable of controlling his own actions. It was then that I set about 'resurrecting' Sir Roger....The solution lay in making a strong impact on imagination! Human beings who have committed a serious wrongdoing are always more or less susceptible to remorse. Even when they haven't confessed, their crime continues to weigh heavily on their conscience, and that situation makes them extremely receptive to suggestions made to them under hypnosis. Inspector Bryce was entrusted with the mission of playing the part of the mysterious new tenant, and I managed to find him a disguise perfectly apt to strike terror into the hearts of any living beings who might be in any way impressionable!...
>
> "I will dare to say," he continued, "that Inspector Bryce managed to make himself look like a creature who was very likely to terrorize and horrify all who saw him!"

That this desired result was being achieved had been indicated earlier in the novel (1.IV):

> All of these successive events, which rained down in their turn on Sir James' somewhat dazed brain, hardly allowed him any time to recover; and it was obvious that, ever since he had asked Burke to conduct this investigation, he had experienced a certain confusion in all his faculties.

In the novel, then, it is Bryce in the vampire role who does so much to make Sir James "impressionable" and "receptive to suggestions made… under hypnosis" – reinforced, of course, by Burke's own efforts within the baronet's household. The premise that disorienting fright will make someone more susceptible to hypnosis is common to all of the versions of *London After Midnight* throughout its variant presentations, whether in the shooting script, the Marie Coolidge-Rask novel, the cutting continuity, or the *Boy's Cinema* fictionization; but it is *least clearly presented in the film (CC) itself* because there the scene (from prior the shooting script) in which Burke explains his intentions to his Scotland Yard superior was deleted. In the film, it is only very late in the story, during the immediate prelude to the re-enactment, that Burke tells Smithson, "Smithson, I'm all ready to prove that when hypnotized a criminal will re-enact his crime." Up to this point the *reason* for his strange actions has not been given.

Of course the hypnotism claim is a questionable premise to begin with; and all versions of the story, in this connection, simply rely on their viewers' or readers' willing suspension of disbelief in order to be entertained. Viewers of the film, in actually seeing Lon Chaney himself in one of his spookiest roles, were probably more willing than most others. Indeed, a climactic moment of the film comes when Chaney-as-Burke takes advantage of the very disorientation and fright caused beforehand by this figure, and *dressed as the vampire himself* he hypnotizes the terrified Sir James as the baronet approaches the haunted mansion.

The problem for the French novel in this regard is this: in the development of its own plot there is simply no need to present Burke himself as ever appearing in the guise of the vampire; and yet the novel's intimate connection to the Chaney film *must* provide *some* presentation of the Chaney character – and not just his assistant – as the vampire. The whole interest of the film to which this novel is tied depends on *that* portrayal *by Chaney*.

Mr. Boisyvon essentially *forces* Burke into the vampire makeup even though his own plot does not require it. Just before the climactic re-enactment of the crime, Burke – appearing "straight" *as* the detective *not* as the vampire (as in the **CC**) – has already hypnotized Sir James *before* the baronet leaves his own house to cross over to the haunted mansion (2.II). The narrative then continues:

> And, allowing the various individuals to act as they intended, [Burke] hurried to the stairs and, running in order to reach the neighbouring dwelling before all the others who were logically due to go there too, he arrived in Sir Roger's residence.
>
> His arrival had been expected.
>
> In the damp and dilapidated front room, **the professor with the silent chuckle seemed to be expecting his arrival**, for he said:
>
> "Ah! There you are, Mr. Burke; I was beginning to get worried at your tardiness."
>
> Burke quickly removed his jacket and hung it on the coat rack.
>
> Then, holding out his hands towards the tenant: **"Quickly, my friend, pass me your Inverness cape and your false teeth."**
>
> "So, everything is going according to plan, Mr. Burke?"
>
> "Yes, **Bryce**, yes, my old friend, and I believe this is going to be the crowning success of my entire career."

Only at this point in the novel, then, does Burke don the vampire disguise for the first time. He then asks Bryce "where is the young lady [i.e., Lucile] whom our loyal Betty brought here?" The narrative then continues (2.III):

> Lucile, just as she had promised Mr. Burke, followed Betty without hesitation and without displaying the slightest fear.
>
> Both women left the house and were admitted into the neighbouring mansion.
>
> And the young woman who was among the new tenants introduced herself:
>
> "I'm the one they call Luna," she said. "You can trust me – please sit down!"

In the novel, then, Lucile first meets Luna alone; the latter is not in the company of the vampire "stranger". Further, Luna does not act "in character" in a way that frightens her as in the **CC**. The novel then goes on:

> "Remember," said Luna, "that you're acting in your father's memory and in order to unmask his killer."
>
> The young woman observed with curiosity the strange appearance of the house in which she had once lived. Those strange black veils, cut into bizarre shapes, hanging from the ceiling – weren't they shaped like bats' wings?
>
> At one particular moment, she shuddered.
>
> She had just heard a voice that was strangely like that of her late father.
>
> But Betty calmed her, telling her she was merely under the influence of an illusion.
>
> She was finally beginning to recover her composure **when the so-called professor came in, and, as she hadn't ever seen him before, she seemed terrified by this frightening figure that had been described to her.**
>
> **But the "professor" hastened to remove his false teeth and mask, and it revealed the face of none other than Burke, for the "transfer of power", so to speak, had just taken place in the hallway.**
>
> "Yes, it's me," said the detective, "and all this is part of our plan. Look at me, Lucile, look me in the eye. I'm going to ask you to allow me to put you into the state in which you were in five years ago."

Burke then hypnotizes her, after which "The detective quickly reinserted his false teeth and readjusted his mask, and, with a brief signal, ordered all present to take up their positions."

What follows is the re-enactment of the murder of Sir Roger, with a couple bizarre additions thrown in by the novelist. First, it is Bryce and not the butler Williams who admits the hypnotized Sir Roger into the house; and the baronet, now believing "it is five years ago" does not notice the anachronistic presence of this new person. Second, Burke in full vampire get-up stands next to Williams when the latter refuses to re-enact his own transaction with Sir James; and "turning towards the killer" Burke recites to Sir James what the detective guesses the butler would have said. Once again, the hypnotized Sir James sees nothing anachronistic in the presence of this bizarre vampire character standing right next to the butler.

The narrative continues with several plot twists, most of them already mentioned, that do not appear in the film itself: an account of the meeting of Lucile and Hibbs inside the murder mansion – both previously hypnotized by Burke – and their separation at the sound of the gunshot; the admission by Williams of his own complicity in covering up the crime; the introduction of financial motivations involving both Sir James and Williams; Burke's revelation that he himself had been in the murder house five years ago, even though no one other than Sir James knew it; and, most surprising of all, Burke's enabling of Sir James to commit suicide rather than face legal consequences or the public shaming of his family. The novelist also subsequently drops what is almost a signature ending to several Lon Chaney films, that his character is shown wistfully watching someone else "go off with the girl" at the end. Mr. Boisyvon's final scene is, rather, a resolution of the relationship between Betty and Harris, which is an invented sequence not in the film.

The point of this section, however, is to note what is probably the major "elephant in the room" of the whole novel: that Burke assumes the guise of the vampire character only at the point when he is about to witness the crime's re-enactment, when there is no need at all for him to don this appearance. To recapitulate: He does not put on the makeup immediately beforehand to confront and further terrorize the weakened Sir James into his hypnotic state, as in the film; and in the novel he has *already* mesmerized the baronet before the latter walks (by himself) to the haunted grounds. Nor does the novel give us any reason to believe that Burke himself has donned the disguise in any previous appearance of the "the old man" with the strange chuckling laugh – it has been his assistant Bryce in that role all along. Nor is it at all *necessary* for Burke, in the novel, to disguise himself as the vampire in order either to hypnotize the susceptible Sir James or to witness the re-enactment of the crime – he does do the former, and could have done the latter, simply in his everyday detective dress. Why then, does he make the last-minute switch of costume and makeup (or "mask") with Bryce?

There are two reasons: first, the novelist's readers must have already been somewhat familiar with the movie, in which Lon Chaney undeniably creates and plays the vampire character – indeed, it is Chaney-as-Burke-in-disguise who appears as that creature on the cover of, and also in several of the still photos bound into, this "ciné-volume" (photoplay edition) itself. Second, the author based his novel on the plot of the film as he actually saw it onscreen – and there, Chaney-as-Burke *does* himself take over the vampire role from his assistant in order to hypnotize the now-susceptible Sir James, and then retains that guise through the quickly ensuing crime re-enactment and arrest of Sir James. As little sense as Burke's assumption of the vampire makeup at this point makes in the novel's own narrative, however, the "Chaney character" that his readers were imaginatively envisioning *had* to appear as the vampire at *some* point.

CONCLUSION

What, then, are we to make of all this? I think the most important thing is simply that the novelist Lucien Boisyvan has provided an entertaining story, and one based on his actual viewing of the now-lost *London After Midnight* film. This is evident in that he follows the basic plot as it was presented onscreen – a plot significantly different from the one given to us both in the original shooting script of "The Hypnotist" by Waldemar Young and in the Marie Coolidge-Rask novelization of that script. Given that the surviving typescript cutting continuity, assembled by editor Harry Reynolds (working with director Tod Browning), is undeniably the best record of what scenes, plot developments, and dialogue appeared in the film itself, the problem faced by the novelist was that he, along with multiple contemporary reviewers of the film, unavoidably recognized that the plot therein – the one that actually showed up onscreen – was simply incoherent. He therefore *had* to fill in gaps in the film's story if he wished to provide a coherent narrative of his own.

His success in doing so, as shown above, is of a mixed character. He did indeed iron out several anomalies and fill in more than a few gaps in the film's story; but he did so in many cases by creating additional problems for his own novel. In his defense, however, it must be recognized that Mr. Boisyvon was a very prolific writer, and to his credit are more than a dozen other novelizations of other contemporary films. It can be justifiably said that much of his career was as a "pulp fiction" writer, and in the heady days of the pulps in the 1920s and '30s terms like "revised draft" and "rewrite of earlier chapters" were not part of such authors' vocabularies. These writers were often paid by the word; speed and volume of production counted more heavily toward their incomes than did perfect coherence in their output.

Part of the fun of reading this novel lies simply in experiencing the rediscovery of a major source connected to "the Holy Grail" of all lost motion pictures – a source that has been just as much lost as the film itself, until now. Lon Chaney fans – of whom I am certainly one – of course realize that there can be no substitute for seeing the great actor moving around onscreen, physically *inhabiting* one or more of his great character makeups. And while we are denied that pleasure in the case of *London After Midnight*, we do nonetheless have multiple sources that at least get us close to what is lost; again: the published shooting script, the photoplay edition novel based on that script, the published pressbook, dozens of surviving still photographs from the film, multiple contemporary reviews of it, copyright registrations, the music cue sheets, the cutting continuity, and the 1928 *Boy's Cinema* fictionization of the story – one that is also derived from an actual viewing of the film. We now also have 'reconstructions' of the film in book form by Philips J. Riley, and in motion picture form (i.e., via panning and zooming of still photos) by Rick Schmidlin. The latter two, however (as mentioned in the Preface) focus mainly on presenting visual retellings of the film, relying mainly on still photographs rather than literary narrative.

Mr. Boisyvon's novelization must now be considered a major addition to the latter group of literary reconstructions, previously inhabited primarily by the Marie Coolidge-Rask novel and the *Boy's Cinema* fictionization.

In sum, though, *all* of the remaining sources give us some fragmentary glimpses of the lost film, like pieces of a broken mirror, each reflecting different facets of what now lies beyond our direct observation. While we may never see the film itself, the rediscovery of another large fragment of that mirror is itself a major cause for celebration among Lon Chaney fans.

Bibliography

Coolidge-Rask, Marie. *London After Midnight.* New York: Grosset & Dunlap, 1928.

——. *London After Midnight.* London: The Readers Library Publishing Company. Ltd., [1928].

"London After Midnight." *Boy's Cinema* (December 1, 1928), 9-16.

London After Midnight, Cutting Continuity, November 25, 1927. Library of Congress copyright documentation, LP25289, Motion Picture/Broadcasting/Recorded Sound Division.

Luz, Ernst. *Lon Chaney in London After Midnight.* Thematic Music Cue Sheets. New York: Cameo Music Service Corporation, [no date].

Mann, Thomas. *London After Midnight: A New Reconstruction Based on Contemporary Sources.* BearManor Media, 2016

——. *Horror and Mystery Photoplay Editions and Magazine Fictionizations: The Catalog of a Collection.* Jefferson, North Carolina, and London: McFarland & Company, Inc., Publishers, 2004.

——. *Horror & Mystery Photoplay Editions and Magazine Fictionizations: Volume II.* BearManor Media, 2016.

[Pressbook for *London After Midnight* (1927). Reproduced legibly in Riley (below), 1985]

Riley, Philip J. *London After Midnight: A Reconstruction.* 2nd revised edition. Duncan, OK: BearManor Media, 2011.

————. *London After Midnight.* New York, London, Toronto: Cornwall Books, 1985.

Schmidlin, Rick (compiler and editor). *London After Midnight* [DVD]. *Lon Chaney Collection,* TCM Archives. Turner Entertainment Company and Warner Bros. Entertainment, Inc.: 2003.

Young, Waldemar. "The Hypnotist." Reprinted in Riley, *ibid.*, 2011 and 1985.

_____ Acknowledgements

I **FIRST WANT TO THANK** indefatigable researcher Daniel Titley, who has spent years researching *London After Midnight* on his own. Upon his contacting me after the publication of my 2016 book on the film, we entered into an email correspondence covering a variety of topics connected with it. Since I collect not just book-format but also magazine fictionizations of old horror films and mysteries, I mentioned to him that I sometimes searched eBay for issues of the French magazine *Le Film Complet*. This popular old periodical, like its American and British counterparts, provided short-story versions of contemporary films in the 1920s and '30s. Although I generally collect only English language works, because of my particular interest in this lost Lon Chaney film I had been hoping to find a French magazine version it, comparable to the *Boy's Cinema* version that formed the core of my previous book. Mr. Titley then alerted me to an eBay offering of the complete *book* fictionization of *Londres Après Minuit* – an entire "photoplay edition" that I had never heard of. I then "bid down" the steep asked-for price of the novel and happily secured its possession. I could tell at that point, from my limited high school and college level knowledge of French, that this story followed the plot of the film's cutting continuity and not that of the shooting script or the Marie Coolidge-Rask novelization. It was evident that here was a very lengthy fictionized version of the story written by someone who must have actually seen the film itself, very close (1929) to its first run.

At that point I felt a real responsibility to share this find with the world's many Lon Chaney fans; but my French was not sufficient for me to do a full translation. Fortunately, a colleague of mine from the Library of Congress, film historian Brian Taves, has been editing a whole new series of Jules Verne stories and plays – those that had gone out of print, or that had never been translated into English at all. And it is BearManor Media that is publishing these works. When I told Brian of my project and that I needed a good translator, he immediately referred me to Kieran O'Driscoll, who had done two excellent translations for this Verne series.

Kieran lives in Ireland, but that distance prove no impediment to his taking on *Londres Après Minuit* as a "work for hire." I think he was as excited as I was at the prospect of bringing this book, for the first time, to the English-speaking world. His translation is wonderful.

So, I most want to thank Daniel, Brian, and Kieran; without all three this book would never have gotten off the ground. But I must also thank Ben Ohmart and John Teehan at BearManor for bringing it into production.

In addition I wish the thank the entire League of Extraordinary Gentlemen, of which Brian is a distinguished member, whose many conversations over meals at Washington's Cosmos Club have urged me on in this task. I have no doubt that whatever royalties I may receive will not even nearly approach what I've already spent simply to acquire the *Londres* book and to have it translated; but having appreciative friends is of more value than royalties anyway.

Printed in Great Britain
by Amazon

49386763R00099